CLAIMING MIA

BJ WANE

Blushing Books

Published by Blushing Books®,
a subsidiary of

ABCD Graphics and Design
977 Seminole Trail #233
Charlottesville, VA 22901
The trademark Blushing Books®
is registered in the US Patent and Trademark Office.

BJ Wane
Claiming Mia
v2

EBook ISBN: 978-1-61258-861-2
Print ISBN: 978-1-61258-908-4
Large Print ISBN: 978-1-61258-909-1

Cover Art by ABCD Graphics & Design

Chapter 1

"Sign here."

With a hand that shook, Mia Reynolds put her signature in the designated lines, effectively ending her nineteen-year marriage on her thirty-seventh birthday. "Is that it?" she asked her lawyer, Bob Temple, who gazed at her across his desk with sympathetic eyes.

"That's everything. This is a good thing, Mia. You can move on now, get on with your life. Why don't you go out tonight and celebrate?"

She gave him a rueful smile. He wasn't the only one pressuring her to move on, or to start going out more. "Maybe. But not tonight. I still have a full day to put in at the nursery and this stop has put me behind." She rose, surprised to find her legs steady since her palms were still damp from stress. "Thanks for everything, Bob. Tell Dee hi, would you?"

"Will do but give her a call. I know she'd appreciate hearing from you."

Mia stepped outside and inhaled a deep breath of New Mexico's warm, arid summer air. Her friend, Dee, wasn't the only person she'd neglected the past year during her separation from Peter. She'd gotten over the surprise and hurt of her husband's betrayal a long time ago, so why had she kept herself so isolated from her friends? Slipping behind the wheel of her truck, she admitted it was the loss of what she'd grown accustomed to more than the loss of her husband she'd missed most when he walked out. Peter had become like her favorite robe, something she'd grown so used to and comfortable with, she never thought of sewing the frayed edges where it had become worn. Losing him hadn't bothered her nearly as much as the shame of him preferring a twenty-two-year-old *skinny* girl wearing a short, silky robe. Now, *that* bothered her.

It took less than ten minutes to reach her nursery and landscaping business located just a half-mile off Whitetail's Main Street. Of course, in her home town of just under fifteen thousand residents, it didn't take long to get anywhere, or for gossip to travel fast from ear to ear. She imagined news of her and Peter's finalized divorce had already spread from one end of Main Street to the other, the same as when they'd split up. Pulling around to the rear of the floral shop and office, she parked and hopped out, waving to her three part-time employees, third-year students from the University of New Mexico, forty minutes away in Albuquerque. She still managed to handle a good portion of the physical work her clients contracted by herself, but valued the manpower and time saved by employing the younger guys. Hiring Barry, Drew and Donny last month after she'd gone full-time with the business had been one of her smarter choices. Hanging on to her dead-end marriage far too long was one of the dumber ones.

Leaning against the truck, she took a moment to scan the acreage of her business and enjoy the fact it was all hers now. Peter had tried to get half of the nursery she'd spent the last fifteen years building up from scratch while he belittled her efforts and goals. She'd been only too happy to remind him how he used to refer to her part-time work as her 'little hobby' and couldn't help grinning ear to ear when he'd taken his first look at last year's financial statement his lawyer produced. Signing over the house where they'd raised their twin sons in exchange for her business had been as difficult as she'd first thought. Priceless memories were stored inside the four walls. It had been the one asset it pained her to give up, but since she had to make a living with the nursery she couldn't afford to give him half the equity.

The boys turned eighteen last spring, and they'd just moved them into the dorms on the campus of Southwestern College in Santa Fe. They'd left small town U.S.A. without looking back and, wide grins splitting their handsome young faces, seemed to take to living in the big city like fish took to water as they wasted no time diving into college by taking a full summer load of classes.

Mia had always been happiest with her hands buried in dirt or in the midst of designing a garden. She never tired of the view of plants and flowers indigenous to her desert state spread out before her; the rows of flowering shrubs and prickly cacti just waiting to adorn someone's lawn or perk up an office front. Dealing with empty-nest syndrome on top of her divorce made her even more grateful for the longer planting and lawn care seasons that came with the extended warm months and short winters of New Mexico. With a sigh, she pushed away from the truck and resigned herself to getting back to the office work she'd neglected this past week, her least favorite part of owning her own business.

She should've known Trish, her part-time office assistant, would be ready to pounce as soon as she entered the building housing the floral and business office. "You're free! When are we going to celebrate?" The perky redhead greeted her from behind the long counter where she stood arranging a wildflower bouquet in a bright blue vase.

"I don't have time to celebrate. Who are those for?" Mia

nodded to the arrangement of white lilies, yellow roses and blue delphinium as she leafed through the day's agenda.

"One guess." Trish's sly grin gave it away.

Mia frowned. "Another one? Didn't he just pick up a plant for his flavor of the month two weeks ago?"

"Yes, but you know how the Chief likes to spoil whoever these gifts are for. I think he enjoys keeping everyone guessing who gets them. Now, speaking of hot guys, I say we hit the bars this weekend and hunt down a man for you to sow some long overdue wild oats."

Mia rolled her eyes at her 'younger by twelve years' employee and friend. "Do you have any idea how long it's been since I did anything like that? I'm way too old to be out picking up a guy at a bar. And I don't need to sow some wild oats. I did that with Pete."

"Mia, I don't know what you did with that loser, but it sure wasn't the down and dirty. If it had been, you'd still be married. There. How's that look?" Trish turned the vase all the way around, checking to ensure the flowers were evenly arranged as Mia taught her.

Ignoring the remark that struck too close to home, she said, "Looks good. When is he picking it up?"

"Soon, so you'll be the lucky one to see he gets it. Tell him I said hi, will you?" She smirked.

Mia sighed in irritation. If there was anyone who could rub her the wrong way, it was their police chief, and Trish knew it. "He always chooses your half day to come by. Another thing that annoys me about the man. Go on, enjoy your afternoon. I'll see you in the morning."

As soon as Trish took off, Mia padded down the short hall to the small office and settled behind her desk to go over the books. Since she'd moved into the compact apartment upstairs, her rent was included in the nursery's bills, which helped a lot on her monthly expenses but was also a large debit she hadn't incurred before the separation. Her bottom line didn't look near as good as the last year before they split. She'd managed to sock away a good sum from her little hobby over the years, but Peter's attorney won that round and half went to the man who was now living with a young woman who was only five years older than his sons. Shaking her head, she vowed to turn over a new leaf starting now and put that man out of her mind. What was done, was done.

Over the next hour, putting aside thoughts of her ex and his bimbo proved to be easier than not recalling a day almost ten years ago that remained seared into her memory. The day she could pinpoint as the beginning of her constant vexation with Nolan MacGregor, the town's bad boy turned law enforcer.

Clutching two filled grocery bags in her arms, Mia rushed out of the store regretting turning down the bag boy's offer of assistance. In a hurry to get home and put away the perishables before picking up the boys from school, she thought she could manage alone, but they were heavier than she'd anticipated. Slowing her steps, she rounded the corner, looked down the street for her car and stumbled to an abrupt halt, the scene before her catching her by surprise. She'd heard Nolan MacGregor was in town visiting his parents, but since she didn't know the man personally, she couldn't get as enthused about one of his visits as most of the female population in Whitetail. She'd never understood her friends' infatuation with the former high school troublemaker who had then gone on to surprise everyone by pursuing an exciting career as a DEA agent in Washington. Yes, he was tall, dark and handsome, but no man had caught her interest since she'd set eyes on her husband eleven years ago.

Not until this very moment as she stood there unnoticed and watched wide-eyed as he fisted one hand in his companion's long blonde hair and brought her up on her toes to meet the forceful possession of his descending lips. Mia's mouth went dry when his other hand latched onto the woman's right buttock, tightened and pressed her pelvis into contact with his. He maintained the masterful hold the whole time he kissed her with a thoroughness that threatened to buckle Mia's knees. Her pulse spiked and a warm flush spread throughout her body when she noticed his butt-holding hand kneading the plump globe through the blonde's short skirt and the way his other hand tightened in her hair as he pressed her against the driver's side of his car.

This is wrong, just plain wrong, *she thought with a rush of panic. She was a married woman, for God's sake, she had no business reacting so strongly to another man she didn't even know. Maybe she'd never felt Peter's hand squeezing her butt or enjoyed such a long, possessive kiss from the only man she'd slept with. She was the lucky one as her strait-laced husband would never grope her on a public street like the uncouth man a few feet from her was doing, oblivious, or just plain uncaring about the people watching.*

And then he did the unforgivable. He raised his head, keeping his hold on the woman as he looked up the sidewalk right at Mia, those razor sharp, enigmatic blue eyes taking in her disheveled appearance with a crooked smile. Mia sucked in a deep breath, the sudden twitch between her legs adding to her discomfort from being caught staring. Irritation replaced mortification and she resumed her step, only to trip over a crack in the walk in her haste to reach her van. Her startled cry as she tried to keep from dropping her groceries resonated in the afternoon air right before a hard arm caught her around the waist.

"I've got you, sweetheart. Here, let me help you with those." Letting go of her, Nolan plucked the bags from her arms before she could stop him. "Where are you parked?" he asked, appearing unconcerned about the glare coming from his blonde companion.

"I can get them," Mia returned, flustered by his sudden nearness.

"I insist." The hard edge to his voice made her buttocks clench, that response as shocking as the one between her legs.

Gritting her teeth, she pointed to her minivan. "There." She dashed ahead of him to slide open the side door, damn near tripping again in her haste to get away from him. "Thank you," she said when he straightened after setting the bags on the back seat. He raised one black brow, the sardonic look as obvious as her prim tone.

"Take care, sweetheart." With a nod, he strolled back to the woman glaring daggers at Mia.

With a mental shake of her head, she climbed behind the wheel and drove home praying she could get herself under control before Peter got home from the office.

Something about the way Nolan had used his body to pin his date against the car, his grip on her head to hold her immobile for his possession, had stirred her in a new, exciting way she still didn't understand. Given everything she'd heard about the man put him as far from being her type as the distance between earth and the moon. She had seen him a handful of times since that day, and quite often since he'd taken the position as police chief, and her reaction to his knowing gazes was always the same. No man except him had ever caused her pussy to twitch from just a look, and because she couldn't pinpoint why he irritated her so much, she blamed it on that anomaly. If she didn't need the business, she would refer him to the florist whenever he called for an arrangement.

Thirty minutes later, she stood reaching for a potted vase sitting on the top shelf in the showroom when the bell over the door pealed. Before she could climb off the short stool, hard hands clasped her waist and lifted her down as if she weighed nothing. Flustered, she looked up, gritted her teeth and shifted in uncomfortable awareness when her eyes met Chief Nolan MacGregor's amused gaze. Okay, she admitted it wasn't the man's physical appearance she objected to. What woman wouldn't look twice at a six foot two, broad shouldered, slim hipped man who wore a Stetson tipped low enough to draw the eyes to the slit of his cobalt blue gaze? No, it was the arrogant dominance he wore like a comfortable coat that put her on edge whenever he entered her place, more so now he was crowding her against the shelves and making her even more aware of that ripped body. She much preferred easy-going, *polite* men.

Wishing it were anyone but him, she stated with a huff, "You're crowding me, Chief."

Those sensuous lips curved in a slow smile as he stepped back. "I wouldn't make you so uncomfortable if you'd let yourself cut loose with me."

Damn. There went that warm flush spreading through her

body when he thumbed back his hat far enough for those enigmatic blue eyes to zero in on her with a long perusal. He made no effort to hide the appreciative trail he took from her braided, dark brown hair to her sneaker-clad feet. How one look from him could make her dormant body sit up and take notice when she didn't even like the man was beyond her. She sure as heck didn't like it. She'd never been one to be ruled by baser urges, instead preferring a positive connection with a man or woman before embarking on a friendship, something that was definitely lacking between her and the chief.

Shuffling behind the counter, Mia breathed a sigh of relief once she put the wide, butcher block space between them. She glanced up, way up, at the only man who'd been able to get under her skin. There wasn't one thing she could pinpoint that rubbed her the wrong way; instead, it seemed to be the uneasy combination of arrogance, dominance and male magnetism she objected to, and her betraying body's response to those undesirable traits. There was no use denying the way her pulse spiked under the slow stroke of his ice-blue eyes that was as potent as a caress, a reaction she should be used to by now since it had been occurring from the moment she first set eyes on him kissing that woman all those years ago.

"Thanks, Chief, but I have enough on my plate right now to keep me from even thinking about being added to your long list of conquests," she returned primly, ignoring his taunting smirk. "Thank you for your order. Trish has it all ready for you." She pulled the vase forward.

"I didn't peg you as the type to listen to small town rumors, Ms. Reynolds." He nodded at the colorful arrangement. "Nice, thank you. I'm glad I caught you in." The way he drew out *Ms. Reynolds* in a slow drawl hinted he knew about the finalization of her divorce. He and every other citizen in Whitetail.

Reaching into his breast pocket, Chief MacGregor pulled out two tickets and slid them across the counter toward her. Tilting his hat back even further, he offered her a better view of his rugged face bronzed by sun and wind and capped with coal black hair tinted grey around his forehead. "You haven't paid these."

"I'm sorry, I've been so busy, I forgot." Picking up the parking tickets, she winced at the fines. Her habit of pulling over and parking wherever it was convenient to expedite her errands resulted in a parking fine more often than not. That was just one of Pete's constant complaints that went along with her always being in a hurry. "I can come in later this afternoon and take care of them."

Leaning on the counter, he replied in that deep voice that never failed to curl her toes. "See that you do. Or, better yet, don't. Now that you're officially free, it'll give me a good excuse to offer you a choice of consequences."

The corners of his mouth kicked up in another smile, but she couldn't miss the hint of a threat behind his words that set her heart to hammering with uncertainty. That didn't concern her near as much as the sudden warm gush between her legs. She didn't even like the man, for pity's sake, and she really didn't care for his forward insinuations.

"What's that supposed to mean?" she asked in irritation.

DAMNED if that prim and proper tone didn't do it for him every time he heard it, Nolan mused, enjoying Mia's flustered look. He'd been lusting after the attractive brunette since first clapping eyes on her standing on the sidewalk, her green eyes round as saucers as she watched him kissing a woman he couldn't even remember by name. When her surprised, flustered look changed to one of curiosity, he'd experienced a tug of interest. But it wasn't until she'd shifted her gaze to his date and he caught a flare of envy that he'd become intrigued. She'd been married back then, which put her off limits, but when he'd returned to his hometown to take a permanent position at the police department, he'd heard about her impending divorce and his captivation with the prickly landscaper had grown steadily in the past six months.

The first time he'd seen her after returning, she'd been bending over the garden bed lining the front of the small police station he'd agreed to take over almost as soon as the offer came across his DEA desk in Washington eight months ago. Her loose shorts molded a nicely rounded, soft backside, and when she spun around at his greeting, the innocent spark of interest in those guileless green eyes and the quick attempt she made to stifle it had pleased him. It was the same look he'd caught on her face that memorable day on the sidewalk.

He tipped his hat down and picked up the vase. "Take me up on my offer of a hot and heavy affair and I'll show you. You know where I'm at if you should change your mind. Put this on my tab, will you?" He walked out, feeling her eyes drilling a hole in his back. The problem wasn't a lack of attraction on her part, he mused as he settled behind the wheel of his cruiser, but fear of what he made her feel.

It had only taken a few bland inquiries of his new staff about the gardener to confirm she was in the middle of a nasty divorce. As he'd settled into his new job, one that promised a quieter pace he'd been yearning for some time, his initial thought upon hearing about her recent split was to continue ignoring the pull she wrought. At forty-three, he preferred uncomplicated relationships with women who enjoyed his dominant proclivities and sexual control. But during those first weeks of acclimating himself to the dynamics of policing a small town and the surrounding low-populated counties, he kept coming across the woman who'd first caught his interest ten years ago.

The more she snubbed his teasing advances with her prim nose in the air and twitched that enticing ass as she turned from him, the more he wanted her. Maybe it was the challenge she presented, or the glimpse of interest he'd caught on her expressive face that kept him interested in pursuing her. He didn't know her ex, Peter Reynolds, but the gossip grapevine reached his ears everywhere he went, and it had been easy to condemn the prick who had betrayed his family for a much younger woman.

Nolan's upbeat mood from sparring with Ms. Reynolds lasted while he stopped in for lunch with his mother and watched her beam over the vase of flowers. No one meant more to him than the woman who had adopted him when he'd been an orphaned toddler and raised him with a strict, but loving hand. His father passed away two years ago, which had been one of the driving factors in his decision to retire from his federal government job as a DEA agent and move back home. He smiled to himself as he now left her house to return to the office. Mia, along with a majority of the town, believed he gifted the plants and flowers to his occasional dates, and it tickled his mother and him to let them think that. Little did they know he hadn't slept with the few women from Whitetail he'd taken out. When it came to sex, he never compromised on his kinks, and therefore stuck with pursuing submissive women for bed partners.

Except when it came to Mia Reynolds.

As soon as Nolan swung into the station's parking lot and saw who was waiting for him in an unmarked car, he shoved aside all thoughts of his prickly landscaper. Sliding out of his police-issued SUV, he didn't spare Chuck Campbell, his ex-boss at the DEA, a glance as he strode inside, tossing over his shoulder, "Let me help save your breath and your time. The answer's no." Letting the door shut in Chuck's face, he nodded to Carrie, the dispatcher, on his way back to his office.

Settling behind his desk, he fumed at the memories seeing Chuck again had conjured up. He had spent ten of his fifteen years with the DEA undercover, forced to sit back and watch one atrocity after another because his false identity and end goal prevented him from stepping in. When the position of police chief opened in his hometown, hundreds of miles from Washington, he'd snatched it up and had been blissfully happy with his choice.

As Nolan knew he would, Chuck followed him into the office, shut the door behind him and held up a placating hand. "You don't have a choice, and it gives me no pleasure to say that." He tossed a photo on Nolan's desk before taking a seat facing him. "Drug overdose, in your jurisdiction."

Shit. Gut churning, he looked down at the photo and swore again. She couldn't have been more than eighteen.

"Best guess, she was between fifteen and twenty. We haven't identified her yet. Third one in two months within a hundred miles of each other. The coroner reports for all three confirmed a heavy dose of tainted cocaine as cause of death." Settling back in the chair, his ex-boss waited with patient calmness that crawled right up Nolan's spine.

Unable to help himself, he glanced down again and winced. It wasn't the worst he'd seen, but bad enough. Pushing the picture toward Chuck, he said, "If it's drug trafficking that's resulted in death due to contamination, and it probably is, that's out of my jurisdiction. Nice seeing you again."

Ignoring him, Chuck forged on. "Nice try. We discovered all three in your counties, which means you're going to help us stop this flow, with luck, before anyone else turns up dead."

Nolan wasn't a hard-hearted son-of-a-bitch, but he had left the DEA for several reasons, one being burnt out on undercover work. "I'm not about to spend another year of my life infiltrating a drug smuggling ring," he warned. "I'll retire first."

"You don't have to, I've got agents ready to slip in if you can lock down the source. We also have a man undercover in Mexico with a known dealer and smuggler. Look, Nolan, I get it, I honestly do. But whether you like it or not, this is part of your new duties as chief. You know what kind of suspicious behavior to look for. If you don't have the manpower, stake out the highway bars yourself. Those dives are always popular for drug transfers and you're new enough on the force no one will recognize you right away."

Nolan fought back his annoyance. So much for trading in his taxing federal job for an easier, less stressful gig. "I left my bar hopping days behind me years ago, but you're right. Those would be the best places to start. I can put a man or two on a rotating schedule, along with myself."

"Contact me with anything, even a suspicion. It'll be more than we have now. It's always been up to us to take over where Border Patrol has failed."

Nolan stood up for the agents willing to take on such a daunting, never-ending task as stopping the flow of drugs pouring over the border. "They can't be everywhere at once."

"I know." Chuck ran a hand through his greying hair. "I'm just frustrated and sickened by the senseless deaths."

"You and me both."

His plans to pursue Mia now she was free had just hit a snag, but Nolan wouldn't let that stop him. He'd just have to find a way to squeeze her in around bar hopping the next couple weeks. He wasn't looking forward to keeping an up close and personal eye on the clubs, but he would do what was necessary to get the tainted drugs off the streets.

Chapter 2

"What is this?" Mia narrowed her eyes at Trish and Dee who stood on the threshold of her upstairs apartment. She was tired and ready for a quiet evening after the busy workweek, although she appreciated the uptick in business that came with the start of summer. Keeping so busy would have helped her set aside the fact she was a free woman for the first time in her life if the friendly, well-meaning residents of Whitetail weren't constantly bringing it up everywhere she went with their solicitous 'how are you's?' She was just fine, damn it, or would be if everyone would let her be. As long as she avoided any contact with Peter and Tami, she could forget the pain of his betrayal, and of losing the home where she'd raised their boys.

And if she could get one domineering police chief out of her mind. She hadn't even seen the man since Wednesday, and here it was, Friday night and Nolan's low, taunting voice still filled her head. She'd just gotten one controlling man out of her life, she didn't need another. Saturdays were her busiest days at the nursery, and the last thing she wanted tonight was to entertain her friends.

"This," Dee announced, breezing past her to toss her purse on the sofa, "is an intervention. You no longer have the excuse you're still married to hide out up here. All work and no play makes you very dull, girlfriend."

Mia closed the door after Trish entered and then eyed the two with a frown. "*You* are married, Dee."

Dee waived an airy hand. "You know Friday nights are Bob's poker night. Unlike the asswipe, Peter, my husband has no problem with me going out for a drink with the girls."

"And, like you, Mia, I'm footloose and fancy free. Now, let's go raid your closet. You can't go bar hopping hoping to score dressed like that." Trish eyed her baggy shorts and sloppy tee with a disdainful look.

"I'm comfortable, which is how I want to spend a relaxing evening *at home*," Mia returned, hoping her wince at Dee's remark didn't show. It had taken the slap in the face of her ex's betrayal to open her eyes to the way Peter had suppressed her life.

Dee padded into the compact kitchen and helped herself to the plate of cookies sitting on the counter. "Do you want to continue giving that man the satisfaction of keeping you where he wants you?"

Mia stiffened. It was true she had allowed her husband to dictate her social life, and she wasn't proud of that now. At the time, his constant referral to her as the mother of his children and her role as the wife of a prominent banker took precedence over gallivanting around with friends. Looking back over the years, she figured she could count herself lucky he hadn't found fault with or discouraged her involvement in her weekly lunch and pinochle group.

"I've been going out," she defended herself now. "Two weeks ago, I went to see that new movie with you, Trish."

The younger girl shook her head as if Mia were a hopeless

cause. "Going to a movie won't get you laid," she returned bluntly.

"Who says I want sex?" Mia's face warmed and she glanced away from the knowing looks they tossed her. Why the heck did Nolan MacGregor's rugged face have to pop into her head whenever Trish mentioned sex? *It's just hormones,* she told herself. Eighteen months was a long time to remain celibate.

"The facts speak for themselves." Dee ticked them off one by one without a qualm. "You're in the sexual prime of your life, have only slept with one man and haven't been with him since, what, months before he left a year ago?"

"Holy shit! Are you freaking kidding?"

Trish's astonishment gave Mia the poke she needed to agree to go out with them tonight. Not because she intended to pick up a stranger, but because they were right. She needed to start somewhere in putting her past behind her. There was no one to blame but herself for allowing Peter to dictate their life together, including limiting their bedroom activity. When he'd thrown the hypocrisy of his constant lectures on maintaining appearances in her face with the truth of his affair, she'd sworn not to let him keep her from living the rest of her life to the fullest, so what was she waiting for?

"I'm not confirming one way or another. What should I wear?"

Both girls let aloud *whoops* before ushering her back to her bedroom. An hour later, Mia stood shaking her head, staring down at her pathetic wardrobe strewn across the bed. She wasn't so old she couldn't recall her teen years and the arguments she'd gotten into with her mother over clothing. Well, there was nothing risqué or too revealing about the garments they'd pulled out of her closet; just the opposite, in fact. Not even a hint of cleavage would show if she donned any of the blouses or tops, and while the skirts might reveal her calves and ankles, there wasn't one among them that would land above the knee.

"This will do." Mia picked up a calf-length sundress that tapered from a snug-fitting bodice to a flared skirt. She'd always liked the way the hem brushed against her bare legs as she walked and how the bright flowers against the white background emphasized her tan.

"*Mmmm.*" Trish tapped her compressed lips with one finger as she eyed the summer dress Mia held up. "Maybe if we leave a few of those top buttons open, that might work."

With capped sleeves and a rounded neckline, the sheath had been one she'd worn to church and out with Peter leaving no buttons opened. Which meant it passed his approval. That reminder sealed it. "Why not?" She marched into the hall bath, ignoring their snickers, and changed clothes. Slipping on a pair of sandals sitting by the front door a few minutes later, she announced, "I'm all set."

"Just two minor adjustments." Dee reached up and flicked open a third button, the one that parted the bodice right at the dip between her full breasts.

Since Mia's best friend's tall, slender build was the complete opposite of her shorter, rounder body, she didn't expect Dee to understand why she preferred not to reveal as much flesh as her friend thought she should. She couldn't decide if it was a good or bad thing Dee didn't give Mia time to debate it. With a tug, Dee pulled the band off the tail end of her waist-length braid and quickly loosened the intertwined strands until the thick mass draped down her back in a heavy, mahogany flow.

Mia scowled as Dee opened the door with an innocent smile pasted on her face. "You know I hate it down. It's too hot and is always getting in my way." The length had been her one, constant defiance to Peter's never-ending complaints about her appearance. He'd wanted her to get it all chopped off from the day of their hasty wedding after they'd found out their one coupling in the back seat of his Chevy had resulted in a pregnancy.

"Make an exception for tonight. Trust me, guys like long hair," Dee returned, waving both Mia and Trish through the open door to prod them along.

"I've got to agree." Trish skipped out the door, swinging her shoulder-length blonde hair.

Mia rolled her eyes and decided it was easier to go with the flow. "You two are impossible." Locking the door, she followed them down the outdoor, side staircase. "Just two drinks, that's all I'm staying for. I have to get up early." Neither said anything, which worried her.

Sliding out of Dee's car thirty minutes later, Mia's pulse spiked with a surge of adrenaline as they walked up to the door of a popular roadside club, hearing music and laughter pumping out. Her one indiscretion with Peter had led to getting married at eighteen and tied down with twins at nineteen, the sudden responsibilities of adulthood shortening her chance to cut loose and explore life like her friends had been doing. The boys remained her one pride and joy, and she wouldn't trade having them for anything, but as she stepped inside the crowd-packed, noisy bar ten miles out from Whitetail, she found herself grateful for Dee and Trish's insistence she join them tonight. She was tired of sitting home alone, bemoaning Peter's infidelity and her own stupidity in staying with him long after whatever had once been between them had died.

Trish pointed across the room and said, "Let's go sit at the bar."

Mia blinked in rapid succession to adjust to the dim interior as her sandaled feet crunched over broken peanut shells strewn across the sawdust covered, worn wood floor. The band perched on a small stage at the opposite end of the room pealed out their version of Josh Turner's, *Why Don't We Just Dance*, while patrons jam-packed on the dance floor tried to two-step in the small space.

Memories of cutting loose at high school dances came

roaring back. She'd been thrilled when Peter, the hot senior and town's golden boy because he'd just won them a state championship in football, had snagged her for a dance. Two years younger, she'd fallen hook, line and sinker for his practiced moves. Watching the gyrating, fast swinging couples, she realized he'd been lacking in the dance department as well as fidelity, only her infatuation had kept her from noticing.

"I'll take a beer," she told the bartender when he made his way over to them.

"Me too." Dee turned to Mia. "Anyone catch your eye yet?"

"I told you, I'm just here for a few drinks." Dee started to argue, but Mia shook her head, picked up her beer and swiveled to face the crowd.

It was too noisy to hold a decent conversation, but she'd always enjoyed people-watching. By the time she downed her beer and held her hand up for another, a pleasant buzz altered her senses. Since she rarely indulged in alcohol, she'd forgotten how fast one drink went to her head, which accounted for how she'd missed the good-looking man approaching with a friendly smile until he stopped in front of her. His slow, appreciative once-over made her itch to place a hand over the gap in her top. Her breasts were among the body parts that had rounded even more from the ten pounds she'd gained since her separation, extra weight she did not need.

Holding out his hand, he said, "I'm Carl. Dance?"

The quick offer sent a warm flush through Mia. After insisting she was just here for a drink with friends, she found herself reaching for his hand with a flare of excitement. It had been a long time since a man showed an interest in her. Chief MacGregor's rugged face popped into her head again, but she shoved his image aside in favor of the friendly, non-pushy man leading her onto the dance floor.

"I'm a bit rusty," she warned him as he pulled her against him.

"No problem. Just follow my lead."

Within minutes, Mia got caught up in the music and her partner's attention. The hot look in Carl's eyes as he spun her about stunned her at first, and worked to give her self-esteem a much-needed boost. She marveled at how fast she had gotten into the swing of things and attracted attention, her smile widening as he twirled her around. *Maybe I should do this more often,* she thought a few minutes later when another man cut in and took her in his arms with an admiring gaze, wrapped an arm around her waist and spun her about.

Laughing, she shook her head, enjoying the feel of her loose hair flipping around and the perspiration inducing movements of her long-neglected body. Before she could break away to get a much-needed glass of water, yet another man cut in, but his crude leer and the cold gleam in his beady black eyes sent a shiver of unease down her spine.

"You here with anyone?" he yelled over the music.

Thankful that she was, she nodded her head. "Yes, I'm with friends." Something about this man made her feel like a bug being viewed under a microscope, and she didn't like it. *This* was the part of barhopping that had worried her.

"They shouldn't mind if you have a drink with me."

Mia didn't care for the insistence behind his tone or the way he inched his hands down to her butt and pulled her closer. She didn't want to sound rude, but she also didn't want his attention. "I'll mind," she returned shortly, trying to pull out of his grasp. When that failed, she cursed under her breath and a frisson of unease slithered under her skin. *Where are Dee and Trish? Why aren't they charging to my rescue?*

THE FRONT LEGS of Nolan's tilted back chair hit the floor with a resounding thud the minute he spotted Mia Reynolds entering

The Raging Bull. *His* Mia. Narrowing his eyes, he took in her loose hair and enticing gap of the top of her dress. He knew women's bodies as well as he knew the illegal drug trade, and he'd spent more than one night fantasizing about the lush curves she tried to hide beneath baggy shorts and loose tops. As much as he enjoyed seeing her in a dress that revealed her shapely calves every time she spun around, he didn't like the way her current dance partner was looking at her. Just what the hell was she up to? The prickly woman he'd been trying to get to know hadn't appeared to be the type to enjoy the club scene. She continued to surprise him, and he liked that.

Seated at a back corner table to better observe the patrons without notice, he watched her skip onto the dance floor, the rapid surge of possessiveness strangling him catching him off guard. He'd been fantasizing about getting that soft, round body under him for weeks. The third man who stepped in to claim her for a dance wiped away his enjoyment of watching her kick up her heels. He'd been keeping his eye out for shady, under-the-table drug deals when apprehension replaced pleasure on Mia's face. Since he much preferred seeing her scowl at him or the uncertain flare of attraction in her green eyes, he deemed it time to step in.

There were a few people he'd spotted during the last two hours of unobtrusive surveillance whom he thought bore watching closer. One of them was the jerk who'd just shifted his hands onto Mia's ass. Striding toward them, he saw her quick scowl, the one his cock always responded to. With a tap on the man's shoulder, Nolan ignored his glare and shouldered him aside.

"My turn." Before Mia could blurt out and call him Chief in front of one of the people he planned to keep a close eye on, he swooped down and covered her startled gasp with his mouth, pulling her up against him as the band switched to a slow ballad.

She stiffened at first, then melted against him, her low moan filling his mouth, her swift surrender taking him by surprise. It took a sharp nip to her plump lower lip to encourage her to open. Delving in, he explored the warm recesses of her mouth with teasing tongue strokes and felt her immediate response in the hardening of her nipples against his chest. He'd suspected his prim and proper landscaper possessed an untapped sensuous streak. Discovering he'd been right prompted him to push his pursuit of getting her into his bed.

ONE MINUTE, Mia was desperate to get away from the jerk who had his hands on her butt and the next, she found herself pressed against Chief MacGregor's wide, thick chest. Her surprise at his unexpected interference caught her off guard long enough for him to settle his mouth over hers in a hard kiss that stole her will and rocked her senses with the way he controlled every second of it. Her body overrode her objections to the man and sank against him, her hands gripping his bulging biceps to anchor herself against his onslaught. A sharp pain lanced her lower lip, startling her into opening her mouth for the sweep of his tongue. Shivers racked her body and drew a low moan that sounded foreign to her ears as he locked an arm around her waist in a tight hold. She couldn't recall a time when she'd moaned over anything sexual, let alone a mere kiss.

Only there was nothing simple about his mouth possessing hers, the no holds barred way he explored her teeth, gums and tongue until she swore he'd mapped out the entire inside of her mouth. He slid his other hand under her hair, cupped her nape and drew her up on her toes to mesh her body even closer to the slow gyration of his hips. The outline of his erection pressing against her mound shook her, a blatant reminder of how many months had passed since she'd had sex.

He pulled back, ran his tongue over the small throb in her lip she could now feel reciprocated between her legs, and whispered in a gruff tone, "Don't call me Chief. I'll explain later."

It took hearing that familiar, deep voice to clear Mia's befuddled, shocked senses. *Crap!* What *was* she doing? No one had ever kissed her like that, with such… possessiveness and control. The sting from that bite on her lower lip seemed to have blazed a trail straight down between her legs if the way her sheath contracted and moistened was any sign. Shock at the easy way she'd yielded compelled her to cover her unexpected response any way she could.

"You're crowding me again."

"Get used to it. What are you doing here? I never pictured you as the bar frequenting type."

Much to her annoyance, Nolan never slowed the swaying of their bodies and she found it difficult to concentrate until his last sentence rubbed her the wrong way. She was tired of being labeled a goody-two-shoes, of doing nothing that might draw negative attention. Peter's constant nagging about keeping up appearances after she'd embarrassed him and his prominent family by getting pregnant had infused enough guilt inside her to make her toe the line her whole adult life. Now, with the boys off to college and her ex making a mockery of everything he'd spent their twenty years together preaching about, she was free to do as she pleased.

"You don't know me well enough to picture me doing anything," she returned coolly, ignoring her pounding heart, sweaty palms and tingling body parts his nearness generated as she attempted to put space between them. "I have friends waiting for me."

The chill that swept her when he nodded and dropped his arms made little sense since she did not like the man. "I would prefer you and your friends stay away from the dives along the highways. There are things going on that we're tracking, which is why I'm trying to lie low as the chief."

"That would mean driving all the way into Albuquerque, as I'm sure you know. I'm a big girl and can take care of myself." Mia spun on her heel and stalked back to the bar where she didn't need to see Dee and Trish's smirks as she slid onto the stool. Nolan put her on edge enough. "Don't say it," she warned Dee.

"I have to. If that man held me, kissed me like that in front of a crowd, I'd be melting in a puddle at his feet." Dee fanned herself, adding in a breathy tone, "*Wow*."

"C'mon," Trish cajoled. "Give. Was it as freaking hot as it looked?"

Hotter. Mia squelched that immediate reply and ignored their probing. "Is this for me?" she asked, picking up the cold bottle of beer. She hoped so as she could use it.

"Yes." Dee sighed in disappointment. "I suppose you'll want to turn tail and run when you've finished it."

"There's nothing to run from, but yes, I'm leaving after this. I have to get up early, remember?" That was her excuse and she was sticking to it, she insisted while denying the need to get away from the probing blue eyes of the first man to wake up her dormant lust. Why did her body suddenly crave the one man she couldn't abide for more than five minutes?

MORNING ARRIVED way too early for Mia as she reached with a blind hand to squelch her blaring alarm at 6:30. Not since she'd been a hormone-driven teenager had she spent an entire night tossing and turning from skin dampening, leg twitching, pussy spasming dreams that left her drained and confused by morning. Sure, she'd read women reached their sexual prime in their thirties, and yes, a year and a half was a long time to go without it, but before last night she'd never experienced such a plaguing itch that left her so needy. It was not a pleasant feeling.

Rolling out of bed with a groan, she padded into the bathroom and brushed her wayward hair out of her face. Shaking her head to clear away the cobwebs of a restless night, she made short work of returning her long hair to its customary braid before bending to splash cold water on her face. Feeling marginally better, she dressed in shorts and a tee, took the time to brew a large, covered mug of coffee to carry downstairs and swore she wouldn't think about the man who played a dominant role in her midnight fantasies.

That lofty goal lasted until she traipsed downstairs and saw Nolan perusing the row of knockoff rose bushes along with one of her best patrons, Clifton Birmingham. The well-to-do landowner had always been a good customer, but it wasn't until he'd contracted with her at the beginning of summer to landscape the entire five acres surrounding his sprawling ranch home on the outskirts of town that he'd become her most elite client.

A quick glance found the guys busy unloading the large flatbed semi that brought in her weekly orders and, seeing no way around it, she strode toward Nolan and Clifton with a resigned sigh. The twitch between her legs the second the chief looked up and peered at her from under the brim of his Stetson didn't bode well for getting through another encounter with him without having to grit her teeth.

"Good morning, gentlemen. Clifton, I have a partial drawing ready, if you'd like to come into the office to look at it." Since she'd told him the entire five-acre plan would take her at least a week to design, she didn't feel bad about putting emphasis on the word 'partial'.

"No rush, Mia." As he had a habit of doing, Clifton reached out and squeezed her shoulder, the look in his brown eyes friendly.

Why his touch always bothered her, she couldn't say, but she shifted away from his hand by taking a step toward a row of small plants with white flowers and rosy pink, feathery seed heads, saying, "These are called Apache Plume and bloom spring through fall, need very little water and direct sunlight. I thought they'd look appealing lining a cobblestone walk up to your porch."

Clifton nodded. "Yes, I like those."

Nolan, damn the man, took advantage of her closer proximity to brush his fingers down her arm, the caress eliciting tingles in its wake. She meant to frown in disapproval when she flicked her gaze up, but her eyes landed on his mouth, and the way the corners kicked up in a taunting grin signaled he knew she remembered the feel of his lips on hers. Fisting her hands, she hissed under her breath as Clifton walked down the row, "Don't do things like that. I'm working."

Nolan bent down and whispered in her ear, "If you'd agree to let me show you what you've been missing, you wouldn't be so uptight all the time."

"I'm only uptight around you," she snapped, the sudden leap of her pulse from his warm breath blowing in her ear as annoying as the man himself.

"You'd be better off asking yourself why that is instead of constantly denying what your body wants." He hesitated and then said the last thing she expected to hear from him. "You're still letting your prick of an ex control your life. Is that what you want?"

Was that what she was doing? She hoped not as that was the last thing she wanted from her divorce. "Is there something you need, other than to harass me?" she asked him, wishing his comment hadn't made her question herself yet again.

He cocked his head and thumbed his hat back enough for her to look directly into his vivid gaze. "Someone should have put you over their knees a long time ago and spanked some sense into you. Keep denying the obvious, and that someone will be me. I'd like four Boxwood shrubs delivered to my place, please." Her buttocks clenched, and her face grew warm as he pulled out a small notepad and jotted down his address. How could he toss out such a threat and then act as if it was no big deal? Ripping off the sheet, he handed it to her with a gleam in his eyes she trusted no more than she did her wayward libido around him. "Later today works fine."

Mia took the paper and watched him stride away with mixed feelings. He tempted her, there was no doubt about that. The question was, why? The whole rugged, domineering, bad-boy image was as far from her type as could be. Then again, she'd only been in one relationship, slept with just one man, and look where her faithful naïveté had landed her. Shaking her head, she shoved her conflicting emotions aside and spotted Clifton talking to the guys by the flatbed. Time to give her best customer her undivided attention.

As she approached them, Drew and Donny were stepping down carrying a crate of Lavender. Barry turned from speaking to Clifton and came around in front of them to greet her. "Morning, boss. We'll have this shipment unloaded by noon. Mr. Birmingham was just asking about the lavender."

"I like the color of them," Clifton commented as he watched Drew and Donny toting the crate of gray-green evergreens topped with violet-blue flowers into the greenhouse.

"Let's go look at my design and see where we can add them." She turned to Barry. "Thanks. Be sure to take a break when you've finished unloading."

"You got it, boss."

Mia led Clifton into her office and spent the next hour going over plans for his acreage, all the while images of her lying across the chief's legs with her bare butt turning red under his hand flitting through her head. By the time they ironed out a few more details and he left, she was so frustrated and confused by Nolan's threat, she couldn't tell if she found the idea of being spanked by him disgusting or tempting. She couldn't deny the more he came around with his blatant insinuations and proposals, the more curious she became about her body's response to a man she didn't even like.

By the time she pulled her truck up to his house later that afternoon, she wasn't any closer to finding answers. Nolan stepped out onto his front porch as she slid out of the truck, her palms again turning clammy and her heartbeat speeding up as she watched him stroll down the drive with a loose-limbed swagger. Even through the denim of his jeans, she could see his thick, muscular thighs contract with each step and couldn't help but compare his muscled build to Peter's leaner frame and find her ex's lacking.

Slamming the door in frustration, she greeted him with cool politeness. "If you want them planted, it'll be Thursday before I can get the guys over here. They're needed at the nursery today."

"I'll plant them. Let me help you unload." He walked to the pickup bed and lowered the gate, his all-business attitude throwing her for a loop.

That is not *disappointment I'm feeling*, she insisted as she helped cart the shrubs to set in front of the porch. "They'll look good along here."

"That's what I thought."

Nolan turned then and shocked the hell out of Mia when he yanked her against him and held her the same as he had on the dance floor last night. With a tight grip on her nape and an arm looped around her lower back, he held her immobile as he kissed her with as much possessive aggression as before. Helpless to fight her body's instant betrayal, she kissed him back, dimly aware they were standing on his front lawn where neighbors or anyone driving by could see them. *Peter would be aghast at such a public spectacle*. Funny how that thought drew a giddy response and worked to spur her on.

Mia was so lost in the taste of him and the thrill of his tight hold tripping up her senses, she didn't notice his lower arm shifting down until he filled his hand with her right butt cheek and squeezed. The startling discomfort followed by a burst of heat between her thighs drew a startled gasp. It took the sound of a car driving by to pull her head out of the clouds and she wrenched her mouth from his.

"You... let me go. People are watching." Her blood heated and a shudder racked her body, but she denied the quick flare of excitement was due to the exhibitionism.

"You worry too much, and care too much about what others think. It only matters what you think, what you want. And I can give you that, but I'm not a patient man, Mia. Decide, and do it soon," he stated in a low tone.

He dropped his arms and she turned her back on his knowing smirk. Striding to her truck, she tossed over her shoulder, "I'll think about it." Ignoring his low laugh response of "You do that" as she slid behind the wheel, she slammed the door and drove off without looking back.

Chapter 3

"Are you going to the Raging Bull tonight?" Mia asked Trish Friday afternoon. Last week they'd had to browbeat her into going out, but she was desperate to put one arrogant police chief out of her mind. She blamed her limited experience with men in general for her reaction to Nolan's two kisses, and the dreams they'd evoked that woke her with perspiration slick skin and a damp pussy. Not even sex with Peter had brought her to such an aroused state, and she couldn't understand how a man who was the complete opposite of her type could affect her with such a strong pull.

"I can't. I'm spending the weekend in Taos with my sister." Trish looked up with a teasing grin from where she sat behind the computer. "Dee and I told you that you would have a good time. Are you hoping to hook up with our police chief again?"

"No," Mia returned so fast even she heard the instant denial in her defensive tone. "In fact, just the opposite. I want to meet someone who is more my type."

"I hate to break it to you, but that man is every girl's type. There are rumors he frequents a club in Albuquerque." At her puzzled look, Trish explained, "You know, a kink club."

A small shiver rippled under her skin as Mia pictured Nolan in such a sex-charged atmosphere, maybe tormenting some poor woman draped over a bench or strung up for his pleasure. She'd heard of such things, and places, but never in her wildest imaginings had she found such kinky behavior arousing. Not until now.

"That doesn't surprise me," she returned in a tart voice laced with disapproval. She was ready to move on, get into a new relationship, and that was all her uncharacteristic musings amounted to. All she needed to do was find a man who had enough in common with her to spark her interest. If she could do that, she knew she wouldn't give Nolan another thought. "I'd rather be with a less intense person, someone who doesn't irritate me every time he opens his mouth."

"Good luck with that. Go ahead and go by yourself if Dee can't make it. The bouncers in the ones I've been to keep a close eye on everyone. I've always felt safe, even when I went alone."

Three hours later, Mia slid out of her truck and ran her clammy hands down the sides of her denim skirt, praying Trish was right. Much like The Raging Bull, The County Line was located between Whitetail and Albuquerque, only a few miles closer to Whitetail than The Raging Bull and off the main highway by a mile. She'd made the snap decision to stop here when nervousness tempted her to turn around and return home before she made an idiot of herself.

"One drink," she muttered as she strode toward the bright red door. If no one caught her interest enough to linger longer, she would leave. With the annual Whitetail summer celebration coming up, she could fall back on those activities to get into the swing of socializing again. The only reason she didn't wait until then was the high risk of seeing Peter and Tami among the town folk enjoying games, competitions and food that brought everyone together. So far, she'd been lucky enough to avoid coming face to face with the young woman responsible for ending her marriage.

The door opened as she reached for the handle and to her surprise, Barry, one of her part-time employees, stepped out with an older, sleazy-looking man she immediately recognized as her butt-grabbing dance partner from last week. She didn't like to judge people by appearances, but something about the other man's cold black eyes and face that revealed ravages of hard living disturbed her.

"Ms. Reynolds! This is the last place I'd expect to see you," Barry exclaimed with an uneasy shift of his eyes toward the other man. "We were just leaving. Uh, the crowd's a bit rowdy tonight, you may not want to stay either."

"Thanks, Barry. I don't plan on staying long. Be careful," she replied with a glance at the other man whose silent staring didn't reveal whether he remembered her or not.

"Always. See you tomorrow."

She nodded and entered the club, intending to give him some motherly advice in the morning. Much the same as last week, loud music and raucous laughter greeted her entry into the club. Unlike last week, she spotted Chief MacGregor seated at the bar right off, the sudden leap of her pulse when she looked that way her first warning of his presence. *Not again*, she groaned. Why couldn't she get away from the man? Her first inclination was to dart right back out the door, but she refused to let him get to her or to put a damper on her fun.

Squaring her shoulders with determination, Mia veered in the opposite direction, sidling along the wall to avoid the rough jostling taking place in the center of the room, and found an empty corner table. She sat in the chair facing the room, feeling more secure in the darkened nook. The snug tank top she'd let Dee talk her into wearing suddenly felt too risqué even though the round neckline only revealed a half inch of cleavage. She breathed a sigh of relief when a waitress stopped and took her order with a promise to be right back with her beer. A fortifying buzz right about now would go a long way, especially since her quick scan of the room made her uneasy. The disreputable-looking crowd of mostly men left her tempted to get up again and leave, but she hardened her resolve to turn over a new leaf by getting out more and trying new things. What could it hurt to stick around long enough for one drink?

Her eyes wandered toward the bar again, but the jam-packed dance floor separated her from a direct visual of Nolan. When he didn't make an appearance at her table by the time she'd turned down two dance requests and was halfway through the cold brew, she let herself relax and order one more. If nothing else, she could entertain herself with people-watching.

Mia finished her second beer and had just decided to leave when angry shouts erupted on the dance floor and all hell broke loose. Within seconds, as if on cue, a melee of flying fists, heavy grunts and grappling bodies that landed on tabletops and upended chairs ensued. Getting to her feet, she tried to make her shaking legs move toward the door, but only managed two steps before a hard arm wrapped around her waist from behind and an angry voice shouted in her ear, "Come with me!"

Recognizing Nolan's deep baritone eased her initial panic, but as he tightened the arm around her waist and lifted her off her feet to haul her out the door pressed up against his body, an unexpected low hum of arousal set up rhythm between her legs. Irritated more by who ignited the unwelcome response than by the inappropriate time and place, Mia wiggled out of his hold as soon as they stumbled out the door along with several others. Mortification over her body's betrayal compelled her to quell the sudden flare of lust with a burst of indignation as soon as he released her.

Hands on hips, Mia glared up into his stern face, barely able to see the blue slits of his eyes under the Stetson. "I'm not a sack of potting soil you can just haul around. That exit was uncalled for."

"I beg to differ," he bit out, grabbing her arm and marching her toward her truck as if she were a recalcitrant child. "I don't know what you're trying to prove by frequenting these dives but stop it. They aren't safe as you just witnessed. Shit, there's no telling what would have happened to you had I not been here." Nolan released her arm and opened the truck door. "Go home, and for God's sake, stay there."

"You're not my keeper, Chief," Mia snapped, incensed by his dictate. She wouldn't let the hint of concern in his voice sway her from her indignation, or the lingering warmth deep inside her core from the feel of all those thick muscles rippling against her much softer frame.

Nolan moved into her, pinning her against the truck with his larger body. Bracing his arms against the hood, he lowered his head until his mouth brushed hers as he spoke in a low growl, "I've decided I am, and the sooner you accept that, the sooner I can give you what you're pining for. Now, behave, and go home."

He moved back so fast, Mia almost reached out to draw him back, the urge to experience another one of his hard, possessive kisses nearly overwhelming her. *I. Do. Not. Like. Him.* Once again, she found herself repeating that mantra over and over as she settled behind the wheel and left the parking lot with a spray of gravel from her spinning tires. She refused, absolutely refused, to glance in the rearview mirror for a last glimpse of the irritating, panty-dampening man.

Mia was halfway back to Whitetail, immersed in her stewing irritation and not paying attention to her speed when the warning wail of sirens snagged her attention off one infuriating, disconcerting police chief. "Crap!" As she slowed and pulled off onto a dirt turnoff, she remembered the parking tickets she'd never paid and swore under her breath. She couldn't afford another ticket on her insurance, or her record.

NOLAN SHOOK his head as Mia peeled out of the lot. The barroom brawl spilled outside in a tangled heap of flying fists and heavy grunts. Unless he wanted to whip out his badge, thus blowing off his chances of spotting any drug deals going down at this place, he'd better take some of his own advice and high-tail it out of here as well.

He didn't know what it was about his little landscaper that drew him with such strong pulls, only that the urge to delve into the interest and need reflected in her expressive green eyes had hit him like a sucker punch that afternoon on the street in Whitetail all those years ago and hadn't abated since. He may have been six years ahead of her in high school and spent over twenty years away from his hometown afterward, but he'd heard about golden boy Peter Reynolds's success on the football field and as a financial whiz, and about his hasty marriage to good-girl Mia Williams. Over the years, he'd caught glimpses of them together, and separately, during his visits back home, and always thought Peter's overblown ego and condescending attitude made him a class-A prick and thought Mia too good for him all along.

It didn't take long after turning onto the highway for Nolan's radar to pick up a speeder up ahead, and instinctively he knew who it was. With a surge of blood-pumping adrenaline, he reached out the window, placed the portable flasher/siren on the roof of his unmarked car and gave chase, not above taking advantage of pulling Mia over to give her a taste of what she'd been pining for without even realizing it. When he came up behind her and she pulled off onto a short turnaround, he thought *perfect* as he slid out of his cruiser.

Turning off the truck, she rolled down her window and there was no mistaking her low groan of feigned sufferance when she recognized him.

"Out of the car, Mia." She obeyed without comment, but even though her vehicle blocked the glow from his headlights, there was still enough illumination around the secluded turnoff for him to detect the rigid set to her stubborn jaw.

When dealing with Mia, he needed every advantage he could get so he didn't hesitate to use her current situation to further his pursuit. Bracing his hands on the truck, he again caged her in and looked down into her wary, defiant face. "Another ticket, *tsk, tsk.* The fines for speeding are a lot steeper than the parking violations you've yet to pay, sweetheart."

"It's your fault," she huffed, crossing her arms as she shifted from foot to foot.

Amused, he drawled, "How so?"

"Never mind. Can't you give me a warning? I can't afford anything else on my record."

Her willingness to negotiate fell right into Nolan's plans, and he allowed a slow grin to inch up the corners of his mouth. Perfect. "How about if I give you a choice between another ticket or a reprimand delivered the old-fashioned way?"

It took a moment for his meaning to sink in, and when it did, her eyes widened in shock and, if he wasn't mistaken, which he rarely was, a hint of curious arousal. His cock twitched at the look on her face and reflected in her eyes, the same one she couldn't hide when she'd watched him kissing another woman all those years ago, the one he'd been obsessed with and couldn't forget.

"YOU WANT to spank me instead of giving me a ticket?" Mia didn't know if her stunned disbelief stemmed from outrage at his audacity or the instant pickup of her heart rate that caused her blood to heat in a volcanic rush through her veins at the thought of his large hand connecting with her butt.

"In the worst way," he admitted with candor, not bothering

to hide the truth. Then again, when had he ever held back from letting her know where his interests lay, she bemoaned.

They both heard Mia's convulsive swallow as she contemplated her choices. It came down to she couldn't afford an increase in her premiums. A shiver rippled down her spine as he pressed closer and his warm breath tickled her neck when he nipped the tender skin. Okay, maybe the strain on her finances wasn't the only reason she was giving his suggestion serious consideration. If she could sate her curiosity about the way her body was always so quick to react to his sexual innuendos about putting her over his knee, remarks she never imagined would titillate her before the divorce, maybe she could put him out of her mind once and for all.

Taking a deep, nerve-bracing breath, she muttered in a whisper, "Fine," as if there might be someone around who could hear her. "I'll meet you… what?" she gasped, incredulous as he spun her to face the truck and hiked up her skirt. "*Here?*"

"No time like the present. Don't worry, Mia, my body is blocking yours, but even if I wasn't, no one driving by can see back in this far." With a hard yank, he drew another outraged gasp from her when he tore off her panties.

Warm summer air wafted over her exposed buttocks for the first time in her life, shocking her when the sudden outdoor exposure elicited a thrill of excitement. Before she could grasp the significance of that, he palmed her right cheek and squeezed, the instant pleasure from his touch taking her breath away.

"Just as I thought," Nolan rasped, bending his head to nip her earlobe. "Soft and malleable. And so very… spankable." He drew back and slapped the same cheek, a light smack that tingled more than hurt.

Mia shut her eyes against the warm dampness filling her long-neglected pussy, mortified by her response to what should have been an abasing experience. The next swat covered her other cheek and was just as potent as the first. Her tense muscles relaxed, and she was just thinking this wasn't so bad when he delivered a harder smack that jiggled her flesh. A small cry slid past her compressed lips, but he didn't give her time to balk or complain as he set about peppering her butt with a volley of spanks, alternating between light and hard enough to sting while moving back and forth between her buttocks. A slow warmth enveloped her entire backside, along with small prickles of pain as the slaps grew sharper. Unable to help herself, she lowered her head to rest on her hands braced on the truck and tried to ward off the escalating pulses spreading down to her sheath. A part of her couldn't believe she was letting him do this and an even more insane part couldn't fathom the escalating arousal the embarrassment and discomfort added to.

Nolan stopped and caressed her buttocks, the now soothing strokes calming her riotous senses. "I knew you had a submissive streak worth exploring," he said in a rough tone.

"I… no, I don't," Mia denied with an emphatic headshake. "I'm only letting… *ow!*" She shook from the blistering swat that seared her backside.

"We can get on with your education a lot quicker if you quit denying what you want, and need," he admonished, his cold voice sending goosebumps racing over her arms.

She refused to go there with him right now, not with her bare butt on display and her pussy quivering from that painful smack. "Are we done?" she asked, already knowing the answer.

"Not hardly."

The smacks resumed, landing harder and drawing a whimper as he struck a tender spot just under the curve of one buttock. Her vagina heated along with her butt and throbbed in tune with the abused flesh. She tried telling herself this was wrong, her response had to be a strange fluke, born of desperation from the humiliating end to her marriage and her celibacy since. Yes, that had to be it, she determined when a blistering smack covered the middle of her whole butt and pushed her hips forward.

"Next time, I'll make you count," he stated with the last, butt jarring blow.

Pent-up air whooshed out of Mia's lungs as the echoes of slapping flesh faded, leaving her heavy breathing and the hoot of an owl the only sounds resonating in the inky darkness. She started to rise but the brush of his hand over her sore cheeks stilled her, as did his next words.

"I can make your body sing in tune with the pain." The graze of his fingers between her aching globes drew another shiver; the light glide over her anus sent a jolt of pleasure and a wave of heat throughout her system. "Let me show you what you've been missing."

"I… I'll think about it." Her brain must be more muddled than she thought for her to even consider an affair with a man she didn't like.

"Just give me one night," he said, squeezing her right buttock before pushing her skirt down. Grasping her shoulders, Nolan helped Mia straighten, turned her around and hugged her. She sagged against him, shuddering, taking advantage of his embrace to gather her wits. "There, all done, and you did fine. Give yourself a moment and I'll follow you home."

"That's not necessary," Mia roused herself enough to protest.

"Yes, it is. Don't speed. Next time I won't be as lenient." With a nudge, he helped her back into the truck, slid her seatbelt on and then kissed her until her toes curled.

The drive home took forever. Every time Mia shifted on the seat, her pussy twitched in awareness of the pulsing discomfort across her buttocks. The sensations that spanking stirred up were all new to her, and she would be lying to herself if she denied being tempted by his offer. She'd always enjoyed sex but couldn't recall a single instance when she'd been as aroused as she was now. Was it the forbidden touch of a virtual stranger, the outdoor exposure and slight risk of exhibitionism, or just plain horniness that accounted for her uncharacteristic response to the chief? She tried imagining herself with one of the nice men she'd danced with last week and couldn't picture allowing any of them to torment her the way Nolan just had. Telling herself she'd let him punish her in lieu of another ticket was a copout, and she knew it.

By the time Mia pulled into her drive, the confusion, irritation and body heat Nolan always stirred up had risen to their highest levels yet. When he got out of his cruiser and followed her up the side stairs to her apartment, her resentment bubbled over.

"I'm perfectly capable of getting inside on my own, Chief."

Ignoring her sniping, Nolan took the keys from her hands and unlocked the door himself. "When you're with me, your body along with your safety are my responsibility, and I take both seriously." Pushing open the door, he stepped back and handed her back the keys. "Give my proposition some thought, but don't wait too long or I may change my mind." Chucking her under her chin, he pivoted and jogged back down the stairs without looking back.

Shaking her head, she went inside wondering what it was about his highhandedness that excited her. Peter had always treated her with polite consideration, sometimes so polite it bordered on aloofness, and she had thought nothing of it.

Padding into the bathroom, she stripped and couldn't help but turn to look at her still tender butt in the mirror. She clenched her cheeks eying the pink tinge and ran her fingers over the tender skin, disappointed to note the soreness was already diminishing. *It's just a fluke, nothing more.* Maybe if she repeated that enough she would start to believe it.

"GOOD MORNING, BOSS," Barry greeted Mia the next morning as she strolled toward where he was stacking bags of potting soil by the outdoor check-out counter.

"Hey, Barry. Thanks for getting this done so soon." She gestured toward the neat rows and then glanced around to make sure no one else was within hearing distance. "Look, I know I'm just your employer, but the man I saw you with last night..."

A hint of impatience crossed his face before he smoothed it out with a smile and a raised hand. "It's okay. We were just walking out at the same time. We'd struck up a conversation at the bar, but other than that, I don't know him or hang out with him. But, hey, thanks for caring."

"My sons are only a few years younger than you. It's hard to suppress those motherly concerns." Even though his frequent tardiness and absences irritated Mia, she still cared about his well-being.

"So, I've gotta ask. What were *you* doing there? I never pictured you for the bar type."

Mia shrugged, annoyed yet another person pointed out she 'wasn't that type'. "There's not much else to do around here, is there? I can only go see so many movies."

Barry laughed. "That's true. But seriously, maybe you should drive all the way into Albuquerque and check out more reputable clubs. They'd be more up your alley."

"I'll think about it. Let's get back to work. Are you guys set on the delivery out to Birmingham's place?"

"Yep, we'll get everything loaded and head out there within the hour. Drew's hooking up the flatbed now."

"Great, thanks. I'll hold the fort down here today so you can get his front gardens in."

Mia returned inside thinking if either of her sons had been so quick to deny any wrong doing, her parental suspicions would kick in. She didn't know Barry, or Drew and Donny that well, and Barry often got under her skin with his tardiness and lame excuses. What they did away from their job was their business. Maybe it was because she fretted over what trouble the twins might court now they were away from home and out from under both her and Peter's thumbs for the first time that she found herself concerned about the young men she employed. Or maybe it gave herself something else to worry about besides the sleepless night due to vivid dreams of a hard-edged cop taking over her body in a way both foreign and tempting to her.

Trish arrived and to avoid questions about last night, Mia quickly assigned her some tasks in the shop before heading back outside to work the Saturday shoppers. Right before lunch, she spotted Nolan turning in and dashed inside, intending to avoid him.

"I'm taking a break. Don't bother me unless it's an emergency," she instructed Trish before holing up in her office. Like the coward she was, Mia waited until she saw him leave again before venturing out.

"What the heck was that about? I could use your help," Trish complained with a questioning look.

"I'm sorry. I… wasn't feeling well and needed to get out of the heat is all. I'm fine now."

"Yeah, right," she returned in derision. "You wouldn't be avoiding our hot chief, would you?"

Rather than lie again, Mia said, "I'll be outside if you need me." Ignoring Trish's chuckle, she got back to work.

By Wednesday afternoon, she'd avoided talking to Nolan three times, but that still didn't put a stop to her sweaty dreams and the empty ache between her legs she'd never experienced before. Not even a session with the vibrator she'd purchased as a pick-me-up gift after Peter left her had helped.

Mia always closed the nursery at 2:00 p.m. on Wednesdays for a mid-week break and, after shutting down, decided to take her mind off her wayward libido by indulging in a shopping trip. Money remained tight, and she needed nothing other than a few groceries, but she loved window-gazing and it was high time she made an attempt to start visiting again with people she'd known her whole life growing up in the same small town.

Funny, she mused as she changed into a sleeveless, knee-skimming sundress and sandals, Nolan was only six years older than her and also spent his childhood growing up in Whitetail, yet they barely knew each other. Once she'd set eyes on Peter, all other guys had ceased to exist for her. She now realized she'd first allowed her immature crush on the popular high school football hero to blind her to his conceited faults, and then his financial success and standing in the community to keep her from admitting neither had been happy for the last nine of their nineteen-year marriage.

Shoving aside regrets, Mia parked in front of her favorite boutique on Main Street and vowed not to let thoughts of either Peter or Nolan ruin the pleasant afternoon. That promise lasted until she entered the popular corner diner two hours later and stumbled to a stop when she almost bumped into her ex waiting to be seated with his girlfriend, Tami. She'd stayed to herself the past year to avoid just such an encounter and her embarrassed fumbling continued when the slender blonde lifted her left hand to her face and a stunning, glittering engagement ring drew Mia's eye.

"Mia, what brings you into town this afternoon?"

The annoyance in Peter's tone rubbed her wrong, but the quick stab of pain when he slipped his arm around Tami's waist and pulled her close stilled her tongue. She no longer loved him, but when she looked away from the smug look on Tami's face and caught others eying her with sympathy, she stuttered a lame response.

"I… needed some things and—"

"Really, Mia," Peter interrupted with disapproving censure. "Your little business will never take off if you're not there to run it."

He'd used that same disparaging tone with her whenever he'd felt she hadn't acted with proper decorum or behaved responsibly. It grated on her now as much as it had when they were married, but when Tami ran her hand down his thigh and he didn't berate her for the public display of affection, it reminded her of how he'd always deemed even hand holding in public as unsuitable for a man in his position.

How could I have been so stupid for so long? Mia squared her shoulders, determined not to let either of them get to her. "Look, I'm doing just fine…"

She trailed off when Nolan came up behind her and wrapped an arm around her waist. Mia had to blink her gritty, sleep-deprived eyes twice to focus past the surprise of his sudden appearance and familiarity. "More than just fine, sweetheart." He held out his other hand. "Peter Reynolds, isn't it?"

Peter frowned, his dark eyes filled with hypocritical reproach as he looked from Mia to Nolan. Taking Nolan's hand, there was no mistaking his wince when Nolan shook it and it was all Mia could do to keep from laughing while enjoying the flicker of appreciation in Tami's eyes as she gazed at Nolan.

"Yes. I heard you'd taken the job of police chief. I hadn't heard you and Mia hooked up."

"She finally submitted to my demands just last weekend, I'm happy to say."

Mia flipped him a startled look, her face heating as she caught his meaning. "Yes, well, he nabbed me at a weak moment."

"Sometimes you have to resort to tough measures to get a woman's attention." Nolan shifted his arm downwards, his hand sliding over her backside in a casual, intimate caress right there in front of the other couple.

Mia started to shift away from the embarrassing touch even as her buttocks clenched in remembered pleasure of feeling his rough palm connecting with her bare flesh. Then she saw the moment Peter recognized what Nolan was doing even though he couldn't see behind her and the flare of indignation on his face halted her movements. Now it was her turn to smirk as Tami's eye's widened and then narrowed. For the first time since Peter had flaunted his much younger fling in front of her, she felt as if she was getting a little payback.

Shrugging, she looked the other woman in the eye and said, "Some men are hard to resist and some," she gazed back at Peter, "aren't."

"I'd rather eat elsewhere," Tami snapped with a toss of her head.

Peter hesitated and then stepped around them. "Chief, nice to meet you."

Without a word to Mia, they left, leaving her standing there in awkward silence with Nolan until she said, "You can release me now."

"Can I?" he murmured just as the hostess dashed up to seat them, her frazzled air explaining the wait.

"I'm sorry for the delay. We got swamped at noon and are just now catching our breath. Two?" she asked, picking up two menus from the hostess stand.

"Yes," Nolan answered before telling Mia, "Don't argue."

Since he was the reason she was gloating from having bested Peter, she didn't complain and let him usher her into the corner booth the hostess led them to. As soon as the girl left, she couldn't help asking, "What was that all about?"

"You let that prick get to you, and it pissed me off. Someday, you can tell me why. And I wanted to show you the effect having an affair with me will have on your idiot of an ex. Wouldn't it be worth it just for that even if you're not convinced yet I can take you places you've never been before?"

Ignoring that last remark, and the shiver his comment induced, she retorted, "How do you know he's a prick if you don't know him?"

"He gave you up, didn't he?"

Mia floundered at that casual remark. How the heck could a man she didn't like get to her with such an off-hand compliment? "Maybe our split was my fault." Hadn't she spent the first six months asking herself what she'd done wrong?

"Doubtful. What would you like? I don't have long before I have to make an appearance at the town council meeting. My treat."

Giving up, which turned out to be easy to do, she ordered a chef salad and told herself she'd rather enjoy a meal with an irritating man who was drawing speculative looks their way than dine alone. She would take the townsfolk's curiosity over pity any day.

"Do you still need time to think about my offer?" Nolan inquired bluntly as soon as the waitress took their order.

"Yes. Don't push me. I've never..." she waved her hand between them, "done anything like that."

"What? Had an affair or enjoyed getting spanked?" he returned with a sardonic lift of one eyebrow.

"Keep your voice down," she hissed, casting a frantic look around to see if anyone heard.

"No one heard me, but you worry too much over what others might think. Remember, I'll only wait for so long."

Chapter 4

Mia's determination not to let Nolan rush her into making such a monumental decision lasted all of two hours following their early dinner, up until the moment she pulled into the bank drive-through to make a deposit. There, against the back door, she witnessed Peter clutching Tami's butt as he kissed her with heated enthusiasm in a blatant, open display smacking of even more hypocrisy than he'd revealed at the diner. For years, he'd refused to even hold Mia's hand where anyone of importance might see them, stating public displays of affection were below his position and unseemly. Granted, he stood with his back to any cars coming around the building and the overhang cast them in shadows, but she could spot his perfectly groomed blond hair and lean build anywhere. And if she could, others could.

Cursing herself and her years of naïve stupidity more than the jerk she married, she dropped off the week's deposit and drove straight to the small police precinct one street over from Main. Slamming out of the truck, she allowed her anger to propel her inside and ask to speak to Chief MacGregor before she could change her mind.

"Thank you," she told the receptionist who, after making a call, pointed to his closed door and instructed she could go on in.

Nolan sat behind a large desk littered with papers, leaning back in his chair with his elbows braced on the armrests and his hands steepled under his chin. Mia hadn't seen him often without his hat on, and the power of his direct, cobalt blue stare hit her with the force of a sucker-punch to the gut and an electric zap to her long-deprived body.

Her pussy went damp, and she blurted the first thing on her mind. "Is your offer still open?"

NOLAN QUIRKED one brow at this quick about-face, reining in the temptation to order her to bend over his desk and accept her punishment for making him wait. Even he knew better than to risk such a thing here. But damn, the longing to do so was nibbling at him with the sharp teeth of a barracuda. She'd pissed him off when he'd followed her into the diner and caught her stammering in front of her asswipe of an ex and his arm candy. Whatever happened between then and now worked to his advantage. He could pull it out of her later.

He jotted his address down and held the paper out to her, his eyes on her face as he instructed, "Come to my house Saturday night, eight o'clock." His gaze drifted down her body in a slow sweep before returning to her pink face and testing her sudden capitulation. "Wear that dress and sandals, nothing else."

"You want me to drive to your place without wearing underwear? In a dress?"

Her appalled tone tickled Nolan, but it wouldn't do to let her see that. "Yes. Any other questions?"

Mia shifted her feet, bit her lower lip, then asked, "Why wait until Saturday?"

"To give you time to calm down over whatever sent you

running here. You need to be sure this is what you want because the one night you are agreeing to spend with me will be done so under my command and your only safety net will be the word red."

Wariness clouded her eyes, but the rigid outline of her nipples through the thin cotton dress and bra gave her away. "I-I can't stay late Sunday morning."

Nolan cocked his head and let his amusement show. "I would enjoy accompanying you to church."

"What? No… that's not… necessary, and not funny, Chief," she added when he smiled.

"I thought it was. I look forward to the weekend, Mia."

"One night, Chief. That's what I'm agreeing to."

"For now," he returned.

She nodded. "For now."

He watched her spin around and leave without another word, her long braid of rich mahogany hair swirling around her rigid back. The woman walked on a great pair of legs, he mused, picturing those rounded thighs clutching his hips or draped over his shoulders. Too bad his own lust would have to wait a little longer to be appeased by her soft body. The one overnight would only leave time for an introduction into everything he could show her, and nothing else. He'd never met a woman her age who was still so naïve about the pleasures her body offered, and he blamed that lack on her prick of an ex.

Over the years, Nolan had gleaned enough about the town's golden boy and his wife through gossip to conclude Peter Reynolds was a self-centered, egotistical asswipe who didn't deserve the years Mia spent with him. Ten years ago, he'd promised himself he would take her over if she ever left her husband. Thank God his long wait was almost over.

His desk phone buzzed, and he reached for it with a sigh. A call coming in on his private line could only mean something occurred that required his personal attention. "Chief MacGregor," he answered, his gut tightening as he listened to the report from highway patrol and wrote down the location of where teenagers had happened upon a body in a field.

"I'll be there in fifteen." *Fuck*, he swore, pushing back from the desk and snatching up his hat after hanging up. Another young person, it seemed, had overdosed on tainted drugs, drugs that likely, if the route traced by the Feds and Border Patrol was correct, had come straight through Whitetail. Whether the victim bought them in Albuquerque or anywhere else was unknown. After leaving orders for two of his deputies, Hank and Morgan, to meet him at the scene, he set off out of town with his sirens blaring.

"Son of a bitch." Nolan fisted his hands as he peered down at the lifeless body of the young man sprawled in the middle of a field, just yards from the busy highway, his sightless eyes frozen on the clear sky above. "Do we have identification?" he asked the highway cop who was first to arrive on the scene. The rancher who owned the land stood off to the side with the three teens, all four appearing distraught.

"Our office is already notifying next of kin and here comes the coroner. Kid's name was Michael Hough, age twenty. Damn waste," the seasoned cop growled.

"It always is. Thanks for tagging me. Tell the coroner to send me a copy of his autopsy report as soon as he can."

"Will do, Chief."

Nolan left Hank and Morgan in charge of taking statements and took long, angry, ground-eating strides back to his vehicle. He had hoped to have a handle on this case by now but had come up with nothing to go on yet. With luck, the Feds' undercover man in Mexico would give them something soon.

"I'VE HAD it with this shit," he snapped into his phone, his gaze scanning the acres he'd owned for over twenty years and intended to keep. "Do something, and do it quick, before another fucking body lands on our doorstep."

"Working on it, boss. There's more bad news," his henchman stated.

"Of course there is. What now?"

A pregnant pause ensued that grated on his already taut nerves before his man relayed the last thing he wanted to hear. "That landscaper saw me with her employee the other night, the tall, skinny kid."

"Barry?"

"If you say so. Anyway, it was all innocent enough, but thought I'd better mention it."

"Just be more careful, damn it. I don't need any more grief. And find me a new source!"

He disconnected and tossed down the phone, his temple throbbing in frustration over this latest cluster-fuck. All of this hassle because he'd been dumb enough to invest heavily in dot com stocks. During the first decade following the crash, he'd gone through the rest of his assets while borrowing from every financial institution that would give him a loan. In his desperate bid to hang on to what he owned, he ended up worse off and left with no options except to turn to illegal financial means or lose everything.

And finally, he'd found himself on the winning end of a business decision by getting into the drug trade. Now, if he could just keep the imbeciles he'd been dealing with from trying to rip him off with this bad shit, he could get back to reaping the rewards from his profitable sideline.

MIA KEPT her gaze on the red-orange glow of the setting sun as she slid out of her truck and ran clammy, shaking hands down her sides. The warm evening breeze wafted under her dress and brushed across the sensitive, uncovered flesh of her labia, drawing a delicate shiver of awareness down her spine. Her quick, damp response added to her already heightened insecurity about the unknown plans for the night.

Nolan's adobe-style house matched others on the quiet residential street, the well-tended lawn speaking of hours of diligent maintenance during these dry, hot summer months. The cacti and yucca plants among the summer blooms ensured he would still boast greenery during the cooler temperatures. That positive character trait would add a much-needed check in the pro side of her list of likes and dislikes about the man inside if nerves weren't crawling under her skin. Being kept in the dark about his plans for tonight had made the last three days the longest of her life.

Every time she found herself waffling over whether to go through with agreeing to this, she shored up her resolve by recalling the satisfying thrill of Peter's face when Nolan had touched her in the diner. If that failed, her startling response to the pleasure-pain of his smacks last weekend was never far from her mind, or the constant curiosity about where it could lead. With a deep inhale, Mia strode up the walk and rapped on the front door.

"Right on time. I like that," Nolan greeted her, holding the door open for her to enter the cool, dim interior of his home. She trembled, not because she didn't trust the chief of police, but because she wasn't altogether sure she trusted the dominant man. "What were you thinking?" Taking her hand, he led her across the tiled floor into a great room and over to a leather sectional facing a massive stone fireplace.

She didn't care for his astuteness and retorted in defense of the unease it wrought. "Nothing, why?"

His jaw tightened as he yanked her against him and slid his free hand under her dress to squeeze one naked buttock. The rough denim of his jeans scratched her bare legs and her nipples tingled against the rippled muscles of his chest from the feel of his hand tightening on the fleshy globe.

"When I ask you a question, don't fucking lie to me or we end this now."

Mia went cold at the thought of him escorting her right back out the door. Her apprehension over the unknown didn't outweigh the need plaguing her this past week, or the necessity to assuage both it and her curiosity. "I'm sorry. I'm not used to anyone except my best friend wanting to know my personal thoughts. It's… disconcerting."

"Get used to it. You know I plan to introduce you to BDSM tonight, and I can't do my job well as your Dom unless you're honest with me. Now, what were you thinking?" he asked again.

It was difficult to concentrate with him kneading her backside, but his steady, stern gaze didn't relent. "You probably won't like it, but I was thinking I wasn't sure I trusted you."

"Of course you do. You're a smart woman, Mia. You wouldn't be here if you didn't trust me." He dropped his hands from her and urged her onto the couch by pressing her shoulders.

Mia thought about those simple words while watching him stride over to a bar in the corner and pour a drink, and realized how true they were. No matter how much he had piqued her curiosity or stirred her dormant lust, she never would have turned to him a few days ago if she harbored any doubts about her physical safety and well-being. Damn, he was good.

Nolan returned to hand her the glass half-full of amber liquid. "What's this for?" she asked, taking it from him.

"Courage. Not that you'll need it, but it can't hurt." He sat down and scooped her onto his lap as if she weighed nothing. "There, that's better." Sliding his hand under her dress, he pushed her thighs apart and skimmed his fingers up the inside. Mia sucked in a breath and jostled the whiskey when Nolan rested his rough palm between her legs and asked bluntly, "When was the last time you had sex?"

The direct inquiry astonished her, but his calm patience as he waited for an answer settled her disquiet. She supposed it made sense he would want to know certain details about her sex life. Now, if he'd just move his hand, she might be able to think straight and come up with an answer that wouldn't mortify her.

Instead, Mia's inner muscles contracted as Nolan put pressure against her pussy and a quiver of damp longing surged deep into her core. Her eyes snapped up to his face as her body shook in response and his steady gaze threatened her composure. "My divorce just turned final," she bit out in defense of her long celibacy.

Nolan sighed. "I really need to do something about that attitude of yours." Keeping his eyes leveled on her face, he drew his hand back and cracked his palm against the soft flesh of her labia. Mia's stunned cry resonated around the room and her attempt to close her legs against the burning sting met with the thick barrier of his muscled arm. "That wasn't an answer, it was an evasion. Want to try again?"

She struggled to swallow past the lump lodged in her throat as his other arm tightened around her waist. Her sheath quivered, and her nipples puckered as the tingling between her legs spread upward. "Not since months before Peter and I split at the first of last year. Satisfied?" She tried squirming against the growing arousal distracting her but calmed when she met with the resistance of his tightened hold.

"For now." Tilting the glass to her lips, Nolan ordered in a tone not to be denied, "Finish it."

Mia downed the last two swallows, relishing the fiery burn down her throat and the warm alcohol fuzzy that loosened her tense muscles and taut nerves. She didn't care for hard liquor but tonight embraced the quick, courage bolstering effects. "Now what?" she inquired, hoping he would stop asking questions she didn't want to answer and get on with whatever he had planned.

"Now," dropping his arms, he nudged her up, "I introduce you to my playroom." Snatching her hand again, Nolan tugged her down the hall, Mia's newly awakened happy places heating up as she padded behind him.

"Playroom?" He stopped at a closed bedroom door and turned the handle. Injecting humor into her voice as she tried to cover up her sudden unease, she teased, "What do you have in there? A kid's jungle gym?"

His lips quirked at the corners. "No, but the idea has merit."

As he flipped a switch on the wall to his right, four corner sconces lit with a bright yellow glow, casting just enough illumination around the room to make out the furnishings that turned her mouth dry and prompted her to protect her vagina by tightening her thighs.

"Is this where you entertain all your dates?" Mia squeaked as she took in a padded bench with a kneeler in one corner and a hanging webbed swing in another. But it was the floor to ceiling poles positioned a few feet apart and centered in the room that kept her rooted in the doorway. She didn't think she wanted to know what the narrow, padded table in front of them was used for. Did she? It was hard to know for sure since her body kept going hot and cold and the low hum of arousal he always induced kept overriding the anxiety churning in her stomach.

"The women I've entertained in here weren't dates," was all Nolan said as he ushered her inside and pointed to the corner contraption with dangling side lines. "That's called a fucking swing. Lots of fun once you get used to it, at least that's what I've been told." He nodded toward the bench. "A spanking bench, self-explanatory. Or would you like a demonstrated explanation?"

Her buttocks clenched and before she could pass for now, he

shook his head with a low laugh that curled her toes. "Never mind. I have something else in mind tonight."

NOLAN COULDN'T RECALL the last time he'd enjoyed a new sub so much. He didn't know if it was Mia's pleasing innocent naïveté or the challenge to replace her bad memories with mind-boggling new ones that pulled the most on his dominant side. Reaching behind her, he unzipped the sundress and tugged the straps down her arms until it pooled at her sandaled feet. Her expressive green eyes flared with excitement, replacing the caution she didn't try to hide as he rubbed his knuckles over her puckered nipples.

"What…" She paused to clear her throat. "What're you going to do?"

"Whatever I want, unless I hear you say red. If you're unsure about something but don't want me to call a complete halt, say yellow. Don't worry," he assured her with a slow glide of one finger up the damp seam of her pussy lips, "I promise you'll enjoy it." She blushed when he held up his glistening finger. "You already are, and I've barely touched you." And that boded so well for the evening, he knew his good intentions to hold off on fucking her could be in jeopardy. "Slip off your shoes and come over here."

Expecting her to obey, he padded over to the poles then faced her as she bent down to unstrap her shoes, her full breasts swaying, the turgid tips dangling downward for a few seconds in a tempting pose he enjoyed. When she straightened, her already red face heated more as she walked over to him. He could read her unease at her nudity in her eyes but was confident he could get her to not only relax when naked but enjoy parading around bare before him.

"Just what are these for?" she asked, looking up and down the poles, her eyes shying away from the attached cuffs above and at the bottom.

"Tormenting wary subs." Nolan guided her between them and nudged her feet apart. "I'm assuming you and the prick never played 'tie me up' games."

A giggle escaped her and loosened her stance enough for him to stoop down and wrap the right cuff around her ankle. "Not hardly," she admitted, pleasing him with the truth.

"Some day you can tell me what you ever saw in him, and why you stayed so long."

"My boys," Mia returned without hesitation.

Nolan looked up to catch an expression on her face he'd seen numerous times on his own mother's, one that told him how much she loved her children. "They're why you stayed, not what drew you to the asswipe in the first place. How does that feel?" Pushing to his feet after securing her left leg, he cupped her face and waited until the sudden flare of panic when she went to move her feet died down. "That's my girl," he murmured in approval as her white-knuckled grip on the poles eased.

"Women like this, huh?"

"Yes, and you will too once you let go of your preconceived ideas of what's right and wrong, acceptable and not."

Her slim brows drew together in that frown of annoyance that always amused him. "How'd you… never mind," she sighed.

Nolan chucked her under the chin. "You're learning, sweetheart." He cupped her full breasts and kneaded the soft flesh before grasping her nipples and pinching as he stated, "Tonight, though, I'm starting with punishment instead of pleasure."

"What? Why?" Mia released her grip on the poles when he freed her nipples and slapped her palms over the reddened buds with a disgruntled glare. "Now what did I do?"

"Two things now," he stated before turning his back on her and padding over to a wall cabinet. "The first was making me wait so long to get you here. Your scowl just now, the second."

After retrieving several items from his stash of toys, he faced her again and watched the wariness re-enter her widening eyes as he carried them over. God, he loved that look.

MIA DIDN'T KNOW which item disconcerted her the most, the black silk blindfold, the paddle, or the thin rod with a plume of short, red and white feathers at one end and multiple, thin latex threaded strands about seven inches long on the other. It wasn't until he laid the items on the odd table in front of her that she saw he also held a pair of wrist cuffs.

"Part of your wait was your insistence on the three-day delay after I agreed to give you one night," she reminded him as her breathing turned shallow. "Does that mean I get to take that paddle to your butt?"

"Since I'm not the submissive one, no." Walking behind her, he took her right hand and buckled the leather cuff around her wrist before doing the same to the left and then drawing both hands behind her and clipping them together.

Mia yanked on the restraints, testing them as she had her ankles. Only this time, instead of panic gripping her by the throat, goosebumps rose across her skin with the skim of his fingertips over her buttocks. She sucked in a breath as he glided those skilled fingers up her sides until he cupped her shoulders.

"Lean over the table, Mia," Nolan instructed, his deep voice a whisper in her ear she couldn't refuse.

Guiding her down, he aided in ensuring the surprisingly comfortable high bench hit below her breasts, leaving them to hang down like ripe melons. The position put her entire backside on display and exposed both orifices in a way that sent heat flooding her face as she pictured him behind her.

Shifting her hips, she groaned, "Nolan…" *Swat!* "*Ow!* What was that for?" she shrieked, flinging her head around to glare at him for the unsuspecting smack that inflamed her right buttock.

He yanked on her braid and grinned. "To divert your attention from your unease. Five more. Count and thank me after each one."

Before she could balk at that order, he brought the paddle down again, delivering a matching heated pulse on her left cheek. Mia refused to give him a reason to add to her punishment and uttered, "One, thank you."

Throbbing pain blossomed across her backside with the next, more forceful blow. It took a few moments for her to talk through her shuddering breaths before she huffed, "Two, thank you."

Bracing for the next swat, Mia jerked when, instead of the expected burn, she felt the soothing caress of Nolan's hand over her hot cheek. A lone moan slid past her compressed lips, the unaccustomed sound once again surprising her. She'd never made noises when naked with Peter. Then again, her ex had never brought her to such a heightened awareness of her body, nor had his touch produced such a pleasurable pulse between her legs.

Nolan shifted his hand down and brushed a calloused finger over her folds. "Your body is ready to embrace a new avenue of pleasure, even if your mind is still balking at the idea. You like domination as well as a light touch of pain."

He didn't give her time to respond before swatting her again. She counted and thanked him, but what she wanted to do was beg for relief. By the time the tortuous spanking ended, her pussy throbbed in tune with her blazing buttocks. He uncuffed her hands and she itched to assuage both aches, but embarrassment stilled her hands along with the sudden darkness when he wrapped the blindfold around her eyes.

"You'll do better with this next part if you concentrate on just the sensations." As he lifted her right arm above her, she felt the soft lining of another cuff tightening around her wrist.

"Tonight's all about new beginnings, starting with new sensations." After he'd secured her other arm, she stood posed in a wide V, left vulnerable for whatever devious, sensual torture he planned next as he shifted to stand in front of her.

"Oh," Mia breathed on an indrawn breath as light brushes of wispy feathers teased her nipples, the soft caresses both pleasant and arousing. She didn't experience the same riotous effect as when Nolan had pinched them earlier, but she wasn't complaining, not when he stroked over her quivering abdomen and then up between her spread legs, tickling her swollen labia. He ran the feathers down one leg next and then up the other before she felt him stepping behind her again. A soft tickling sensation ghosted across her buttocks, the effect tugging on her clit and making her sheath twitch.

"*Nolan.*" She wasn't sure what she was pleading for, only that she ached in ways that were new, a touch uncomfortable and a lot frustrating.

"I wanted you relaxed before I did this."

Mia jerked and cried out from the abrupt switch of soft caressing to the fiery snap of supple leather wrapping around her hip, the lines of stinging heat different yet igniting the same response as the paddle and his hand. Alternating between light swats that teased and warmed and harder strokes that stung and burned, he worked the flogger over her buttocks and down her thighs with practiced precision. She didn't know whether to breathe a sigh of relief or moan in frustration when he stopped and ran the leather strips around her stomach and trailed them across her breasts. She relaxed into the softer strokes as she tried to reconcile with the pulsing lust he seemed intent on ignoring. Her body was full of surprises, and she cursed the years she'd been ignorant of its potential as she shook in the bonds and waited in darkness for the light of pleasure.

"Nolan, please," she begged when he brushed the strands back and forth across her turgid nipples. She could feel her cream dripping and knew he could see what he was doing to her.

"I love hearing a woman beg." Nolan nipped the tender spot where her neck met her shoulder before snapping the flogger across her breasts, hitting both nipples at once.

Mia arched her back, her nubs puckering into such tight tips they hurt. She heard him drop the flogger and then his hands were on her flesh, kneading, tormenting her further. He drove her to mindless ecstasy when he added his mouth, scorching her skin wherever he touched, kissed, nibbled. Fingers plucked at her tips, lips and tongue soothed the ache. Hands skimmed down her waist, fingers delved between her legs, stroking, teasing… plunging. He drove her up on her toes with a deep thrust then made her insane with want when he milked her clit only long enough to begin the soft pulses of an impending climax.

She cursed him in a low, frustrated voice and he laughed. She writhed between the poles, trying to maneuver toward his roaming hands and mouth, and he scolded her. She whimpered and pushed back when he breached her anus with two slick fingers and he praised her. She went rigid and then convulsed with the shocking tsunami of ecstasy his mouth on her clit released, and his deep groan vibrated up her vagina.

The tugs on her clit from Nolan's lips and teeth lit up the darkness behind the blindfold into the most astonishing, mind numbing, body consuming burst of colorful pleasure. Mia thought the waves engulfing her body would never end as he drove her from one orgasm to another without giving her time to catch her breath, let alone deal with pleasure she never dreamed possible before tonight. Tears leaked from under the blindfold as her perspiration-soaked body shook. With her mind clouded by the heights to which he'd driven her, she fell against him in a boneless heap as soon as he released her bonds and whipped off the blindfold. She felt the give of a soft bed, heard the rustle of clothing and then only had a few moments to enjoy coming into contact with warm skin stretched over taut muscles before succumbing to exhaustion.

I'M A FUCKING SAINT. Nolan fisted his raging cock in one hand while holding Mia's lush body next to him with his other arm. He'd gone into tonight knowing it would be all about her, as it should be when introducing a new sub to the benefits her body craved from domination. But in his over twenty years of experience as a Dom, he'd never been so tempted to say to hell with what was right and ravish the girl who had entrusted herself to him. Frustrated, he squeezed his dick, trying to relieve the pressure, but all that did was increase the pounding flow of blood to his groin.

Giving up, he stroked his shaft with rough jerks, the image of Mia's pink-striped body egging him on. He would face a different woman come morning, he knew that. She would awake with doubts, with recriminations, and in denial. He'd seen all of that crossing her face during the hour he'd kept her restrained between the posts. He'd also heeded the shock of her arousal reflected in her eyes when he'd lifted her torso from the bench; heard the stunned surprise of her body's response to his torment in her voice as he used both the feather and flogger on her; and caught the tears when her body convulsed with pleasure under his hands and mouth, intense orgasms he doubted she'd ever experienced before. None of that fit in with her good-girl image or matched her responses to the man she'd promised herself to for years, the man she'd thought she loved.

He knew Mia and had seen how intimidated she'd let herself become by her husband's betrayal. It pissed him off whenever he thought about it and swore the next time he caught her cowering from the prick and his haughty bitch, he'd do more than fondle her ass right then and there and wouldn't care where they were or who saw.

Nolan's palm grew slick as he cupped his cockhead and smeared pre-cum down the rigid length of his erection. He needed to get to sleep so he was alert when he faced Mia's insecurities in the morning. Tightening his fist, he yanked on his rigid flesh until his release shot up from his balls and spewed across his stomach, the orgasm loosening his taut muscles but doing little to calm his lust.

Chapter 5

Mia stumbled into the attached bathroom in Nolan's bedroom on wobbly legs the next morning. She'd caught a whiff of coffee after waking alone in his big bed, and the much-needed gift of caffeine prompted her to hurry. Daring a glance in the mirror, she cringed at the sight of her mascara-streaked face and puffy lower lip. She retained a vague memory of sinking her teeth into her bottom lip once or twice out of sheer frustration and need, and once to keep from sobbing over the explosive climaxes she'd been missing out on.

That wasn't me, she denied with a shake of her head before leaning over to splash cold water on her face and rid herself of the proof of her debauchery. *It'll take more than clearing away smudged makeup to do that.* "Shut up," she told her reflection before snatching a royal blue hand towel. She needed to get home, take a long, hot shower and lose herself in gardening chores. She didn't doubt she could put last night aside once she immersed herself in the work she loved and stuck with the friends she *liked*.

After finding her dress draped over a chair and her sandals on the floor next to it, she slipped them on and swore her pussy *was not* twitching and that *was not* anticipation rushing through her veins as she padded down the hall and into the great room. Her reaction when Nolan glanced across the room from the kitchen and snared her with his probing, blue gaze proved she was in denial.

"Just in time. Sit down." He nodded toward a small round table in the corner. "I have omelets almost ready. How do you take your coffee?"

If he could act blasé this morning, so could she, Mia vowed, crossing the space as she replied, "A tablespoon of creamer, if you have something other than powdered."

"I do. Tell me how you're feeling this morning. Any problems?" The casual tone behind the question belied his intent perusal, something she couldn't get used to.

Flustered, she sat down and sipped from the mug he set in front of her before answering. "I'm fine." After he brought over two plates her stomach let out a loud rumble. "I guess I worked up an appetite," she mumbled, red-faced.

"I guess you did."

Mia's mouth watered when she looked down at the cheese-oozing omelet with peeks of fresh spinach and bacon filling. "Oh, wow. I think I'll come here for breakfast instead of the diner next time I want to eat out." It took only a second to realize what she'd said and have her stammering, "I mean…"

Nolan laughed. "Relax, Mia. You're welcome here anytime, for a meal or anything else you… crave."

She halted her fork halfway to her mouth, frowning at his wording. "I… this was a onetime thing."

A pang gripped her chest when he shrugged, surprising her with the hurt that indifferent response wrought. She'd have to remember he had gone the whole night without wanting her enough to ease his own lust. It would be in her best interest to let the lesson she'd learned from Peter's betrayal stick.

"That's your choice, but I doubt you'll be happy going back

to your celibate lifestyle, not now that you've experienced the benefits you can reap from submitting to the right man."

"I was restrained, not submitting," she returned, piqued at his comment.

"Is that the excuse you're giving yourself to condone the way you came apart under my tutelage? Did you convince yourself that what you did wasn't right for a woman to not only indulge in, but enjoy?" he taunted.

Her face warmed under the hard censure to his tone and how prudish his words made her sound. She didn't like coming across so prim and proper all the time but couldn't break a lifetime of habits overnight. Uncomfortable with his scrutiny, she retorted the first thing she thought of in defense. "You can't judge me since you didn't… participate."

Nolan almost choked on his omelet and reached to grab his glass of orange juice to swallow it down before asking, "Participate? Is that your polite phrasing for fuck?"

Mia couldn't help it. Her lips twitched with humor that matched his. Okay, that had come out wrong, but he rattled her, so, of course she blamed him. "For some reason, I turn into an idiot around you. That's probably why I don't like you. Nothing personal, you understand."

"Oh, sweetheart, I understand you perfectly," he drawled. "Are you finished?" He nodded toward her empty plate.

It surprised her to look down and see she'd devoured the omelet. "Yes, thank you. It was wonderful."

"Glad you liked it." Shoving his chair back, he ordered, "Turn your chair to face me."

WARINESS DREW Mia's frown again, but she nonetheless did as Nolan instructed and scooted her chair around to face his. Another lesson was in order after that denial of submitting, and he enjoyed demonstrating his points. Patting his thighs, he said, "Drape your legs over mine." He waited calmly while her eyes widened and sparked with a flare of excitement even though she fisted her hands in her lap in indecision. With a sigh of resignation, as if she didn't have a choice, she lifted her legs and rested them across his thighs, her dress hiking up with their spread. Trailing his hands up the soft insides of her legs, he pushed the hem even higher as he asked, "That wasn't so difficult, now was it?"

She sucked in a breath when he reached the crease between thighs and hips and slid his thumbs inward to rub over her already glistening folds while keeping his gaze on her face. "Harder than you think," she gulped, her face turning pink.

"If you're unsure, put your hands behind you and clasp them together while you decide if you want me to continue." It didn't surprise Nolan when she complied without hesitation, but he knew better than to smile. Dipping his right thumb past her slick seam, he teased the warm, soft side of her vaginal wall as he spoke. "Tell me why you stayed with the prick for so long. It's obvious you two weren't suited."

Mia's thighs tightened alongside his arms, but she didn't struggle against his hold, only in defiance of admitting the truth. "We were… well, at one time. I… *oh, God*." A visible shudder shook her body when he grazed her clit.

"You what?" Nolan inched further inside her, pressing against the spot he'd located last night that was sure to elicit another spate of moisture… right… there. He fought a smile when she creamed his digit with a warm gush and her slick walls tightened.

"Huh? I don't want to talk about my marriage." Her jaw went rigid and those expressive green eyes snapped, but she made no move to disengage herself from her position.

"Fair enough." He cocked his head. "Do you want to come?"

Mia's rosy face darkened to a deep red at the blunt question, but he maintained eye contact with her while continuing to slide his thumb back and forth between her clit and her sweet spot, putting just enough pressure on each to keep her teetering right on the cusp, with small contractions of her slick walls clutching at him.

"I… of course I do. How could I not, with you…" She looked down between her legs, where he kept one thumb buried inside her while still caressing the sensitive crease between leg and crotch with the other.

"Then ask me, nicely. Say, please, Nolan, may I come?"

Shaking her head, she bit her lower lip and lifted her hips into his marauding hand. Nolan pressed harder inside her, pumped deeper before circling the swollen, tender bud over and over, waiting… waiting…

Mia's glazed look of pure need changed to resignation before she leaned her head back, closed her eyes and pleaded in a soft whisper, "*Please*, may I come?"

Instead of answering, he plucked at her clit, pumping the bundle of nerves until the second before she convulsed. He with-drew and tapped her pussy hard enough to deliver a small sting and watched her explode with a startled cry of release before returning to milk her clit through her orgasm. She was stunning when she climaxed. He loved watching her body shake, her breasts heave, and hearing her small cries that indicated she was experiencing something that was still new.

He caressed her thighs as she came back to earth by slow degrees, her eyes opening to reveal glazed stupor before changing to stunned disbelief at her response. Lifting her legs down, she stood and smoothed her dress, turning away from him to look around for her purse.

"I have to go. I open at one," she said with a catch in her voice.

Pushing to his feet, he pointed to the small table next to the sofa. "Your purse is where you left it last night."

"Thanks. I'll see you around."

"Mia." Nolan waited until she turned from the door, leaving her hand on the knob as she looked back at him. "You weren't restrained this morning." He saw the moment his words registered, and their meaning sank in.

The disdainful look that always stirred his cock entered her eyes. "I guess you showed me, Chief."

"I showed you the truth about yourself, Mia. What you do with it is up to you, and yes, you'll see me around."

She left without another word, but Nolan didn't intend to let this be the end of it, of them. He'd given her enough last night and this morning to think about, had successfully shown her what she'd been missing and craving without knowing it. The scene last night had been mild for him, but just right for a newbie. He'd tempered his use of the paddle and flogger so as not to scare her off with harsh pain, putting enough strength behind the strokes to make her ache for more and then arousing her with the feathers and his hands and mouth.

He would give her today to assimilate everything she now knew she would respond to and then pester her for more, not yet ready to give up on her.

MIA WAS STILL SHAKING when she pulled away from Nolan's house, and she couldn't blame all of her trembling on the explosive orgasm that erupted from that stinging slap on her tender flesh. As if that alone hadn't been enough to grapple with, he had to toss out that last remark, the one that forced her to reevaluate her thinking about her responses to everything he'd done to her.

Sex had never been more than a mild, pleasurable release at the end of a busy week raising two rambunctious boys. Until Nolan had touched her for the first time. She went damp again just remembering the feel of his hands and mouth and those wicked props of delicious torture. And then to follow up this morning with that short but effective eye-opening scene in his kitchen… she honestly didn't know where to go from here. Now she had a myriad of confusing, conflicting emotions to deal with on top of a body still vibrating from the touch of a man she didn't even like. Her mouth ticked up in a rueful smile as she wondered what her response to Nolan's dominance would've been like if she harbored a fondness for the man. At one time, she'd loved Peter, but couldn't recall a single instance when she'd come apart during sex like she had with Nolan.

It's because of my long dry spell, she insisted as she entered the nursery lot just shy of opening time at one. That would have to suffice as an explanation for her wayward, uncharacteristic actions for now and she prayed no one found out about her one night of debauched excess. Another truck rolled through the gate behind her and she got out and waved to Drew and Donny, frowning when she saw Barry wasn't with them. The temperature was already climbing, and plants needed tending.

"Where's Barry?" she asked in a sharper tone than she'd intended. It wasn't the first time he hadn't shown up or had come in late.

Drew fidgeted, flicked a quick glance toward Donny and replied, "He's tied up with something but will be here, boss."

"He swore he was only running fifteen minutes behind," Donny added.

Mia blew out a frustrated breath and gave them her stern 'mom' look. "I'll deal with him when he arrives and remind him to let me know when he's running late. You two start watering while I get the deliveries lined up."

Sunday afternoon shoppers tended to browse more than buy, but she couldn't afford to be shorthanded if that proved different today. She was coming out of the greenhouse twenty minutes later, waving to Dee and Bob who were looking over the row of annuals, when Barry came strolling toward her with a sheepish grin.

"Sorry, Ms. Reynolds. I was doing a favor for someone and didn't keep track of the time. Won't happen again."

"You made that promise before, Barry." With her wristband, she wiped the sweat from her brow, not liking the way his jaw clenched even though he kept the small smile in place. "One more time and you're gone. Go help the guys." She walked away before he could blow his last chance with an insolent remark.

She'd just finished ringing up a customer when Dee bounced up and grabbed her arm, her Cheshire grin setting off Mia's inner alarm before she even heard Dee demand, "Okay, give. I heard your truck was seen parked overnight at Chief MacGregor's house."

Mia groaned over the pitfalls of small hometown living. "Who told you that?" she hissed, after making sure none of the browsing customers could hear them.

"Barb Willis at church this morning. She lives two houses down from him. You lucky hussy, I want details."

With an emphatic shake of her head, Mia refused to reveal what went on between her and Nolan. She was still assimilating through everything she'd experienced, everything she'd felt, and what Nolan hadn't done or explained this morning. He'd pursued her until she'd caved and agreed to the overnight he wanted, yet the way he'd held himself back still both baffled and upset her. She didn't understand him, his motives or what he wanted from her, and didn't care for the emotional rollercoaster ride he'd left her stranded on.

"No, and don't ask me again. I mean it," she warned when Dee opened her mouth to protest. "It was a onetime thing, not to be brought up again. Got it?"

"If you insist," Dee agreed with a huff before touching Mia's tense arm with a look of concern. "If he upset you, though…"

"He didn't." She hesitated for a second before offering her

best friend something to ease her mind. "It was great, Dee. I'm just sorry I didn't know how good it could be before now."

Dee started to comment but saw her husband, Bob, approaching with a flat of the bright green-leafed, red flowered perennial, Pineleaf Penstemon Mia knew Dee wanted for ground cover. Grateful for his timing, Mia reached out, took the wooden crate from him and set it next to the register.

"Good choice. If you plant them where you can see them out either your front or back window, you'll be able to enjoy the hummingbirds they attract," she informed them as she rang up the purchase without looking at Dee. Mia should have remembered how pushy her friend could be.

"We'll talk later," Dee whispered as Bob swiped his card.

Ignoring her, Mia smiled at them both. "Are you two going to be at the annual picnic this year?"

"Of course." Bob grinned. "We haven't missed one yet. You'll be there this year, right?"

Mia shrugged. "Sure." After her bumbling reaction to facing Peter and Tami at the diner, she changed her mind about going this year and planned to skip the gathering the entire town turned out for, not wanting to face them again. She intended to come up with an excuse to appease her friends before then.

"Good. We'll hold you to that." Bob's smug look matched the one on Dee's face as she finger-waved goodbye.

"Catch you later, Mia."

Mia blew out a breath of exasperation. Why did she have to be lucky enough to have such good friends?

The afternoon sped by and she was grateful for the business that kept her mind off both Nolan and Barry's disgruntled attitude, at least until Nolan showed up five minutes before closing. Her heart executed a slow roll as he unfolded his six-foot-two frame from behind the wheel of the police-issued cruiser and tipped his Stetson down to shade his eyes from the late afternoon sun. His loose-limbed stride ate up the ground between them and the way his thigh muscles bunched beneath the snug denim of his jeans drew a sheen of perspiration along her neck that had nothing to do with the summer heat. The tight stretch of his black tee shirt across his shoulders and around his biceps emphasized his bulging muscles, and she shivered as she recalled the comforting strength of his arm wrapped around her as he drove her crazy.

And all she could think was, what more could he want from her?

"I'm about to close, Chief," she managed in a cool tone despite the instant flutter of her pulse and deep in her core when he stood in front of her.

"Then my timing is perfect. Let's get something to eat."

Mia stiffened and took a physical step back from the temptation to say yes she didn't understand. "I don't think that's a good idea. Thank you anyway."

He unnerved her with his silent scrutiny before he drawled with a tip of his hat, "Good enough, sweetheart. For now." Without another word, he pivoted and returned to his vehicle, leaving her standing there bemused, irritated and… needy.

"We're out of here if you don't need anything else, boss," Donny said, his approach drawing her attention away from Nolan's departure.

"No, thanks. I'll see you at the end of the week."

Barry was already driving away as Drew joined them. "When are you expecting another delivery? We can arrange to be here to unload if it arrives before Thursday."

"Thanks, Drew, but I've slowed down on ordering since planting season is ending soon. I have a small shipment due in three weeks, a lot of fall shrubbery. Now I'll need your help most for the weekly lawn services and the landscaping contracts."

Drew nodded. "Works for me. See you Thursday afternoon then."

It had been great of the guys to pick the summer school

schedule that could give them the most hours at the nursery. Whenever Barry annoyed her, she remembered how hard they always worked between Thursday afternoon and Sunday evening.

Mia closed the gates and trotted upstairs to her apartment, eager for a hot shower, cold salad and quiet night, vowing to forget about a certain police chief who could tie her up in knots with just a look. She didn't even like the man, for pity's sake.

THE MAN she didn't like but who could still seem to send her blood flowing in a hot molten lava flow of pulsating need with just a look or his nearness, intercepted her in line at the grocery the next morning. "I'll get those for you," Nolan insisted, his tone indicating he wouldn't take no for an answer.

Instead of arguing in public, Mia hissed, "Fine," none too pleased as she followed him out to her truck. "I didn't need your help." She glared at him after he set the bags on the seat.

"Not with your groceries, but you do need me. You're just too stubborn to admit it. You'll like a club I belong to in Albuquerque. Let me take you there this weekend."

Leaning his muscled forearm on the top of the truck's door, he stared down at her with a small curl of his mouth and made her long to feel those lips crushed to hers again. Shaking off the unwanted desire, she replied, "I don't think that would be a good idea. Thank you anyway."

His small grin stretched into a smile. "Good enough, sweetheart. For now."

MIA HAD JUST PLACED her foot on the first stair to her apartment on Tuesday, intending to break for lunch while Trish manned the office, when Nolan again showed up out of the blue. She paused, waiting in annoyance for him to reach her carrying a takeout bag from her favorite taco shop.

"Chief. What can I do for you today?" She knew her voice dripped sarcasm and didn't care. The tacos smelled too darn good.

"Have lunch with me." He snatched her hand and she let him tug her over to the covered picnic table behind the shop.

"I should file harassment charges against you," she grumbled, taking a seat and the taco he handed over.

"But you won't. It's lingerie night at my club on Saturday." He bit into his taco, his eyes never leaving her face.

"That's nice… just what kind of club is it?" she asked around a throat gone dry.

"BDSM, kink, alternative lifestyles… pick a name. I promise it's safe, sane and everything is consensual, no different from my house last weekend."

Except he would want to torment her in public. No way, no how, even if her traitorous body went damp at the image in her head. She swallowed her bite, took a long drink of bottled water and replied, "I don't think that would be a good idea. Thank you anyway."

He didn't argue, instead switching to mundane topics until she took her last bite and he stood to gather the trash. "Good enough, sweetheart. For now."

Mia watched Nolan saunter back to his truck, scowling at his back. She needed to do something to neutralize the increasing urge to agree to his invitation yet one more time.

HE DIDN'T MAKE an appearance on Wednesday, and she wasn't happy when she caught herself looking for him, refusing to admit to disappointment.

On Thursday Barry called in sick, so it was left to her to do the mowing at the police precinct, another aggravation to plague her. Her mood didn't improve when her palms turned clammy and her heart thumped with expectation when she saw Nolan's vehicle in the parking lot. When he brought her a bottled iced tea, invited her to his club again, and it was on the tip of her tongue to say yes, she knew she needed to do something to get her mind off him.

"I don't think that would be a good idea. Thank you anyway," she answered automatically. This time, Nolan left her unsettled when he deviated from his standard reply.

"You'll be sorry when I stop asking, sweetheart."

That's what worried Mia.

NOLAN ENTERED the Raging Bull on Friday night in a foul mood. His third bar that night, and he had spotted nothing that would point him toward nabbing the people smuggling the tainted drugs through his county. On top of that frustration, Mia's stubborn refusal to let go of her insecurities and get on with her life was wearing thin. Maybe he'd made a mistake in not fucking her last weekend, he contemplated as he slid onto a barstool and held up one finger to get the bartender's attention. Considering her inexperience, he'd believed a slow initiation into what she'd been missing and suppressing her entire adult life would be best. For the first time in a long while, he might have handled a sub wrong. Not that she'd admitted to being submissive.

With a curse at not being able to get a grip on her, he ordered a beer and swiveled around to face the crowd, this one tamer than the last two. Too bad. He was in the mood for a fight. And then Mia walked in, fidgeting with the short hem of her denim skirt, Trish yanking on her arm to lead her to a table.

The look on her face appeared more resigned than happy to be here, and he guessed the younger girl had talked her into coming. His first inclination was to storm over there and haul her outside for another lesson, but he reined in that urge to do his job.

An hour later, Nolan was ready to call it a night, and to drag Mia out with him. She'd done nothing since coming in but sit at the table and drink while watching Trish flirt and dance. By his count, she was on her third beer and he decided it was time to tell her she wouldn't find what she craved in alcohol.

Coming up behind her, Nolan reached around and plucked the beer bottle from her hand before she reached her mouth again. "You don't need this." Setting it on the table next to hers, he sat down and faced her angry glare. "You will not forget last weekend, or what I can do to and for you, so give it up," he growled in demand.

"That is not what I'm doing," she snapped, shifting in her seat.

"Sure it is. Why else would you come here and just sit?"

Mia opened her mouth to reply then clamped it shut again before releasing an exasperated huff.

Leaning back, he crossed his arms to keep from reaching for her. "Talk to me, Mia. After the way you came apart under my hands and mouth, why are you running away from me instead of begging for more?"

Mia flicked a panicked glance around before relaxing and leaning forward. "How did you know I would… like what you did?" Not even the dim lighting could disguise her blush.

"I've been a Dom a long time, sweetheart. I've learned to read women well, and you are an open book."

"Dom? As in women kneeling at your feet and calling you Master?" Her voice emerged in a whispery gasp, but those stunning green eyes glowed with interest.

He nodded, his mouth quirking. "As in. My dealings with

suppressed subs has proven they're the ones most responsive to dominant control."

She reared back as if insulted and said exactly what he thought she would. "I'm not suppressed." Nolan noticed she didn't deny being submissive, so he raised one brow and just stared at her until she fidgeted and snapped, "Knock it off."

"Careful, sweetheart," he warned, deepening his voice. "I have ways to punish you you may not enjoy as much as a spanking."

Mia tilted her head, curiosity replacing censure on her face. "Like what?"

He shook his head, bemused. She never failed to surprise him, and he liked that. "Like hours of orgasm denial."

A SHUDDER RAN THROUGH MIA. After her explosive climaxes last weekend, denial sounded like pure torture. So why did her body tingle from head to toe at the thought? She mentally shook her head, glancing away from Nolan's penetrating gaze. She'd let Trish browbeat her into coming tonight in the hopes someone would take her mind off him and his invitation. *A sex club*. Just the words threatened her resolve to stay away from him. Curiosity and a week of low, simmering, unfulfilled need that his actions last weekend seemed to have stoked higher instead of appeasing made her itch to say yes. And then he said the one thing sure to get her to agree.

"How long are you going to allow Peter, the prick, to keep you wallowing in regret? Come with me tomorrow night." He held up a hand. "We'll just observe, more only if you want. C'mon, Mia. What have you got to lose except time?"

Before she could change her mind, she listened to the heated clamoring of her body and said, "Yes."

Chapter 6

Mia ran trembling fingers through her unbound hair as Nolan grabbed her other hand and led her up a stone walkway leading to the stately, two-story home surrounded by five acres of well-kept, landscaped lawn. The man saw way too much without her revealing visible signs of how his attentive nearness always flustered her. It had been that way ever since that chance encounter on the street when she'd experienced a warm rush from witnessing his dominant control for the first time. As a married woman, she'd had no business feeling anything for a man not her husband, and contributed her startling, unwanted response to her instant dislike. Even though she was now free to indulge in another relationship, she still couldn't wrap her mind around the way he tugged at all her senses.

"This isn't what I expected," she commented as Nolan reached for the ornate doorknob and pulled open one of the doublewide doors.

"A BDSM party can be anything from a small gathering in someone's private home to a crowd of over a hundred members indulging at a downtown club." He nodded inside the wide, marble-floored foyer. "A group of us went together to purchase this place to give us something in between the relaxed atmosphere of a spacious home with the strict rules and oversight of a well-run establishment."

He kept a tight grip on her hand as she brushed by him upon entering the mansion. Faint strains of edgy music filtered through the walls along with laughter and the low hum of conversation. Nolan tugged her to the left and down a short hall that opened into a high-ceilinged, spacious room where about twenty people were enjoying a drink and the long table of appetizers. Other than the women dressed in a variety of sexy lingerie a lot more revealing than the torso-hugging, spaghetti strapped camisole and short skirt Mia wore, she noticed nothing like what she'd expected. Something of her surprise must have shown on her face because Nolan stopped and peered down at her with a wry twist to his lips.

"Disappointed or relieved to not see people engaged in sex?" he asked in a slow drawl that sent a wave of heat through her.

"I didn't know what to expect," she defended.

"There are theme rooms on the second floor and private rooms on the third. We'll explore those shortly." He drew her toward a corner bar. "You're allowed one drink. What would you like?"

Mia almost stumbled when a command from a stern-looking man sent his attractive companion to her knees in front of him. Releasing his erection into her hands as the couple they'd been conversing with watched, the young woman appeared unabashed and content to use her mouth to lavish attention on his shaft.

"I think I'll have a rum and coke," Mia replied when she could talk past her dry throat. Watching such an open display of eroticism and the pleasure consuming the young woman's face made her even more conscious of her bare buttocks bisected by the miniscule thong Nolan had insisted she wear, along with dictating the rest of her outfit.

Lifting her by the waist onto a barstool, Nolan grazed under her chin with his knuckles. "I never said members didn't indulge in this room."

She crossed her legs, hoping to contain the sudden dampness seeping between her pussy lips. Ignoring his last statement, she thanked the bartender for the drink right before the distinctive sound of a hand slapping bare flesh drew her attention across the room. Long blonde hair obscured the face of the woman who lay bent over the arm of a sofa, her naked, reddened butt put on display. When the man swatting her cheeks paused and rested his hand against one bright crimson globe, her wiggling hips stilled, and her legs relaxed. Mia took a fortifying drink, relishing the immediate warmth from the strong liquor as her buttocks clenched in response to the memory of her similar reaction to Nolan's hand on her backside.

Nolan nodded toward the couple as he reached for his beer. "That's Mandy and her husband, Alec. I've known them for about ten years. Nice people. I'll introduce you later. Let's check out what else is going on."

"I'm good down here," she protested when he helped her off the stool.

"But I'm not. Come on."

Mia blamed his hard tone, the one that brooked no argument and never failed to send a delicious shiver rippling down her spine for the way she fell into line as he steered her toward the wide, curving staircase. Gripping the cold glass as if it was her lifeline, she downed another swallow when they arrived on the second floor and the sound of leather snapping against skin followed by a high-pitched, exalted cry echoed down the wide hall. Nolan didn't help calm her nerves when he slid a hand under her skirt and pressed against her naked buttocks to prod her into the first room on their left.

She almost dropped the glass when Mia saw the scene taking place and it was only Nolan's quick rescue when he plucked it from her hand that saved her that embarrassment. *I definitely need to get out more,* she mused, gazing wide-eyed at the naked woman sprawled on the middle of a dark walnut, boardroom-length table. Her perspiration-damp body writhed under the restraining hands of one man holding her arms above her and two shackling her ankles, keeping her legs spread wide apart for a fourth man to feast at her pussy. Another woman lay bent over a desk in the corner, her partner wielding a wooden ruler across her bright crimson-lined, quivering backside. Feminine cries resonated around the dimly lit room, the mix of pain-filled yelps and screeches of pleasure indistinguishable.

Leaning against the wall, Nolan pulled Mia back against his chest, sliding his hand from her buttocks to palm the flesh between her legs. "This is the Executive Suite, for obvious reasons," he whispered in her ear while pressing his middle finger between her folds just far enough to graze her clit. "I'll bet you never imagined watching could be as titillating as indulging."

It was difficult to concentrate on his words or the two scenes with his calloused finger circling her nub, teasing her with light touches before retreating to brush her juices over her labia. A man seated across the room from them leaned back in his chair with his arms crossed, his dark eyes never staying still, including her and Nolan in his constant sweeps of the room. Mia's curiosity got the better of her and she leaned her head back on his shoulder, looking up at his sun-bronzed face as she asked, "Who is that?"

"Master Gary, the room monitor. The Masters take turns rotating throughout the night, making sure the house rules aren't broken."

The man's presence and Nolan's explanation made Mia feel better. She relaxed even more against his hard frame and closed her eyes while trying to urge his hand into more action with a thrust of her hips. The quick pinch he delivered to one fold drew a groan of frustration and a sheen of sweat along her arms. Opening her eyes, she meant to turn a glare on him, but instead got pinned by Master Gary's gaze. Nolan took advantage of her sudden stillness to slide his arm from around her waist and reach up to lower one strap far enough to scoop out her right breast. With a warm flush, she found herself responding as much to the other man's heated look as to Nolan's thumb strumming her nipple.

Nolan's deep, amused voice in her ear spread goosebumps over her damp skin. "I love the way you continue to surprise me, sweetheart. Public exposure can be as much fun as watching, can't it? If you deny it," he added when she hesitated, "I'll bend you over the desk next to Megan and ask Master Chase to use his ruler on you."

Mia blanched and shook her head. "Okay, yes, it seems I'm not opposed to… a few things around here."

"Good enough this time. Watch them." He followed that command with a finger-stroke down her dripping seam and over her anus as Master Chase rolled on a lubed condom, spread Megan's glowing cheeks and pushed with slow insistence past her tight rim. "I will fuck your ass one day soon, and you'll love it."

Mia didn't know if her shaking was due to the potent carnality of viewing the other couple or Nolan's words uttered with threatening promise. He didn't give her time to think about it before dropping his arms, picking up her hand and escorting her back out to the hall, leaving her teetering on the razor-sharp edge of climax.

Pointing to an open door, he said, "That's the Wet Room."

Curiosity once again overrode her frustration, and she entered the next room with an eager step. Large fans whirled above, drawing the billowing steam from a bubbling whirlpool and the row of open showers up and out of the room. With the walls painted a light blue above murals of seashores and the sound of waves splashing ashore being piped through hidden speakers, it would be easy to imagine yourself on a beach. Mia was too busy ogling the couples in the showers to be embarrassed by her still exposed breast. They didn't linger, but she knew she wouldn't mind spending time naked in that room with Nolan.

"Now where are you taking me?" she grumbled, wishing he would opt for a private room next. If he ended tonight without fucking her, she knew she wouldn't give him a third chance. She could only take so much of this. It may have taken a lot of cajoling from her friends and pressure from Nolan to get Mia out of her shell, but now that she'd caved to him again after enjoying a taste of what she'd been missing all these years, she found herself eager to explore everything. If he ended up holding back from her again, maybe she would like one of the men she'd seen tonight more than him. There weren't any who couldn't draw a response from a woman with just a look.

"One more theme room, this one similar to mine at home." Nolan opened the next door and her first thought was he was wrong. This space was nothing like his at home.

The only light came from the four corner wall sconces flickering an orange-yellow glow along the walls. There were more people in this room than the other two, putting to use each apparatus, including the dangling chains along one wall. Mia cringed and inched closer to Nolan when a whip-wielding Dom struck the smooth back of a woman bound facing a large padded X. The sub jerked and cried out, but when the Dom thrust a finger between her legs and withdrew glistening proof of her arousal, Mia knew she was a willing participant

"Don't even think about putting me up there and using a whip on me," she couldn't help but warn Nolan in a hissing whisper.

He frowned and yanked down her left strap, releasing her other breast into his hand. "First, I was remiss in not telling you to adhere to the proper respect while here, so I won't punish you this time for your tone." With his eyes on hers, he slowly applied pressure to both nipples as he stated, "I'm not into heavy S/M practices and know you well enough to know you're not either.

However, I'll caution you to be mindful of others and tolerant of their preferences."

Mia sucked in a breath from both the reprimand and the slight pain numbing her tips and zinging south to her pussy. Eyes watering, she leaned into his hands, biting her lip to keep from pleading for him to release her. She hadn't meant to come across as judgmental, but she heard it in her tone nonetheless. "I'm sorry." For some unfathomable reason, her distress seemed to stem more from the heavy weight of his disapproval pressing on her chest than the discomfort he caused her.

A smile softened his face as he released her tortured buds. "That's my girl," he murmured, the simple words easing her chest constriction as the sudden blood flow to her numb nipples elicited sharp pinpricks stabbing into the tender tips. "*Ow*!" Slapping her hands on her breasts, she tried lessening the painful throbbing by rubbing them.

"Oops, did I forget to warn you about that also?"

"Very funny."

The relentless tension of unfulfilled arousal built to an aching crescendo as Nolan walked Mia around the spacious room and treated her to the same torment as the women bound on each piece of equipment. At the spanking bench, he shocked her by lifting her skirt and swatting her butt in tune with the man spanking the woman restrained. With her buttocks burning, they shifted over to a chain station where he withdrew a pair of nipple clamps similar to the ones the woman dangling was wearing and pinched them on Mia's tender nipples. Her throbbing tips pointed the way as they strode across the room to the St. Andrew's Cross where that sub moaned, now bound facing her Dom and enjoying the deep thrusts of his cock. Nolan held Mia in front of him and finger-fucked her sheath, timing his strokes with the other man's, withdrawing before she climaxed along with the other woman.

It didn't take her long to recognize the pleasurable freedom to embrace her responses the club afforded as opposed to the constant worry over appearances dampening her enthusiasm. She could get used to this, she thought, but only if Nolan intended to end her long dry spell from intercourse. With her body humming from head to toe in arousal and shaking on the cusp of orgasm, she rounded on him before he could lead her to the next scene. "I swear, Nolan, if you don't take me somewhere and end this waiting, I'm leaving."

NOLAN YANKED Mia out of the room and pressed her against the wall with his body as he braced his hands on either side of her head and glared down at her. Even though he'd succeeded in getting her to the frustration level he'd been aiming toward, he wouldn't let her insubordination slide.

"That's Master Nolan, or Sir. Last warning." He slid his hands down and pulled on her clamped nipples to emphasize his point.

She sucked in a breath with a whispered reply. "Okay… I forgot again."

He let go of her nipples with a sigh. Her innocent expressions of aroused surprise and her body's blatant responses made him forget how new she was to his sexual lifestyle. Removing the clamps, he bent his head and licked over each reddened tip, her deep inhale releasing on a whoosh as he eased the aches with his tongue before nibbling his way up her arched neck to her mouth.

"You make me forget myself, and that's a first for me, sweetheart." He covered her mouth, pressing his raging erection against her mound as he mimicked with his tongue what he intended to do with his cock very soon. Her low moan of eager acceptance vibrated down his throat and spurred him into moving.

"Come with me," he growled, pulling back and snatching her hand.

"Where are we going?"

Nolan didn't answer, just tugged Mia up to the third floor and into the private room he'd reserved earlier that day. Closing it behind them, he made quick work of stripping her and tossing her onto the bed with a bounce that jiggled her full breasts and elicited a laugh from her. The neatly trimmed brown curls framing her pussy lips glistened with her arousal and when her thighs fell open, he almost drooled like an adolescent at the enticing pink swath of damp flesh waiting for him.

"You should be careful of what you say to a Dom, sweetheart," he said, straddling her waist before lifting both her arms above her head. After binding them in cuffs attached to the headboard, he scooted down and grasped her right leg under the knee. "You could find yourself in a position you can't get out of without saying the safeword. Do you remember what it is?" He pulled a strap over from the side of the bed and wrapped it around her thigh.

"Yes. Red." Wariness entered her green eyes and a blush stole across her face as he tightened the strap enough to pull her bent leg out to the side and then moved to do the same to her left leg. She jerked, the test of the bonds deepening her red flush. "I-I'm not sure about this," she admitted with a look of consternation.

"I am, and that's what matters. If you want to end this, say red. Otherwise, keep quiet so I can play. You present quite a feast, Mia." Nolan ran his hands over her quivering breasts, down her waist and up her spread thighs, her soft skin dampening as he explored her body.

Plucking at her nipples, he watched her eyes dilate. He reached under her ass, noting her increased breaths when he pushed his thumb past her tight sphincter. As he pushed three fingers deep inside her pussy, she gasped and shifted her hips, already begging with silent demands for more.

Nolan leaned over to the end table and withdrew a new butt plug, one he'd placed there earlier. "I have plans to fuck your ass one day, and in order to do that, I need to start preparing you."

"You do?" she squeaked, eying the plug he was lubing with wide eyes. He watched her buttocks clench as he lowered the toy between them and almost smiled at her attempt to stop him. "I'm not sure…"

"For someone who demanded my attention not fifteen minutes ago, you seem to be not sure about a lot." Nolan rubbed the slick, round end of the plug against her puckered hole until it slid inside with relative ease. "Again, safeword or keep silent. Last warning." He pinned her with a stern look before pushing a little harder inside her tight ass. "Not so bad, is it?" he asked when he embedded the entire three inches.

"So, I can talk to answer that?"

With a blistering swat on the inside of her thigh, he admonished, "Cut the sarcasm. Obviously, if I ask a question, I expect an answer." He waited, twisting the plug as he kept his gaze on her.

"No," she huffed. "It's not bad."

"In fact," he palmed the damp flesh between her legs, "I'd say you like it." Using his middle finger, he slid inside her heated pussy and circled her clit, watching her eyes glaze and her breathing grow labored.

With his free hand, Nolan lowered his zipper and released his cock into his palm. "Do you want this? Want me?" he demanded, stroking his shaft as he continued to tease her small bundle of swollen nerves.

"I… yes, *God*, yes," she whispered without lifting her eyes from his hands.

"Fuck, yes," he muttered, making quick work of sheathing himself before kneeling between her thighs and pushing inside the moist, hot silk of her tight pussy. It took patience and his iron will to labor his way into her slowly enough to loosen her muscles sufficiently for her to take his full length. "Shit, Mia. How long has it been?" he ground out when he lay embedded inside her snug warmth and her slick channel folded around him like a glove.

"Too long. Nolan, Sir, please *move*."

Was it any wonder she'd been impossible to forget since that afternoon on the sidewalk of Main Street in Whitetail? "Didn't I just caution you about being careful what you ask for?" Rearing back, he worked his way through her tight muscles again, one tortuously slow inch at a time as he pushed deeper. Her abundant cream helped ease the foray into her hot pussy enough for him to withdraw and slam back in with more force. His thrust rasped over her clit with ample friction to prod velvet-soft muscles into clamping around his rigid length. Tight as a vise, they massaged his girth with unyielding clutches as he increased his hammering assault, pumping his climax forward way too soon.

Mia's thighs tensed against his sides, her struggle to either free herself or get closer drawing a wave of pleasure he relished as much as the gush of cream coating his shaft. He increased his tempo, each plunge jiggling her breasts glistening with a damp sheen, her pinpointed nipples searing his chest until he bent his head and drew one succulent tip into his mouth to suckle. Her mewls of pleasure egged him on, empowered him to go deeper, demand more from her than he had any other woman. Their sweat-slick bodies slapped together as he pounded between her legs, each stroke meant to drive them both toward that precipice of no return.

MIA'S NIPPLES puckered so tight they hurt, feeding fuel to the fire raging below. Nothing mattered but the pounding together of their hips, the forceful thrusts of Nolan's steely cock invading her welcoming sheath, his mouth on her breasts. She sobbed with the build-up of pleasure then screamed as it fragmented her body into a million pieces.

By the time her head cleared, and the powerful aftershocks of her climax dwindled to small pulses, she found herself free of the restraints and butt plug, and Nolan's hard arms wrapped around her still quaking body. Vulnerability settled over her as tears pricked behind her scrunched-closed eyes for no discernible reason. Yes, it had been ages since she'd last experienced the intimacy of sex with a man, but she hadn't been ready until this man pushed his way past the shield she'd erected after Peter's betrayal. Her body still trembled in damp reaction to the stunning heights he'd driven her to, forcing her to admit it was more proof of what she'd been missing out on since she lost her virginity in the backseat of Peter's car twenty years ago that left her defenseless against the encroachment of sad regrets.

"I have… to get back," she whispered against his hair-roughened chest, the desire to cling warring with the need to return to the stable comfort of her home.

Nolan leaned up and gazed down at her with one of those probing stares that made her want to squirm. And then he said the one thing sure to straighten out her thoughts. "Are you going to let the asswipe continue to hold you back, or will you agree we're good together, and that you like what I can do for you, and," he reached down and flicked one tender nipple with his thumbnail, "to you?"

She stiffened beneath him and his slow smile softened his stern, dark face. "You still want to… see me?"

He chuckled. "If by 'see you' you mean fuck you in ways you've never been taken before, then yes. C'mon, Mia," he coaxed, nibbling on her lips. "What have you got to lose? Let's set the tongues to wagging with an open, torrid affair, one where you agree to my control," he sank his teeth into her lower lip and drew her gasp, "whenever," he licked over the throbbing flesh, "wherever I say."

All it took was that searing look in his penetrating eyes and her quick, hot response to the stinging pleasure of his touch to set her heart to pounding with excitement. Why fight that when she could finally admit she didn't want to? Maybe she would even grow to like him a little if he continued to gift her with such mind-boggling experiences as tonight.

Mia shrugged, feigning indifference even though she was sure he could feel her body vibrating with titillation as she recalled the shocked, hypocritical look of disapproval on Peter's face when they'd been in the diner. No, she didn't want to continue letting him rule her life and keep her from pleasures he'd never shown her.

"Okay, Chief, you're on. I'll agree to giving you control, but for sex only. I won't be a doormat for you, or any man." Looking back, she realized that was exactly what she'd been during her marriage, and just what her husband had wanted.

"Deal." He kissed her, swift and hard before rolling off the bed and hauling her up next to him with a swat on her butt that sent tingles racing down to her core. "I like the way you're not afraid to give back as good as you get, and the way you submit to my demands."

"I feel I have to tell you," she said as she picked up her thong from the floor. "I still can't say I like you. No offense, just being honest." She didn't care for the way his eyes lit with amusement at her bold statement. Snatching her clothes out of his outstretched hand, she snapped, "What?"

"Sweetheart." He nodded toward the rumpled bed. "If that's the way you 'don't like' me, I'll take it."

Her lips quirked with suppressed laughter. He could do that —irritate her one second and make her want to giggle like a schoolgirl the next. Zipping up the skirt, she defended her actions that contradicted her statement. "That was just sex. It doesn't mean anything. Right?" Mia couldn't fathom why she held her breath so tight her chest squeezed as she waited for him to confirm that explanation.

She should have known he wouldn't make it that easy for her. Instead of addressing her comment, he took her elbow and led her back to the stairs. "You have to get back, remember?"

Huffing an exasperated breath, she ignored the tight clutch around her heart. Since she didn't care much for him, it was just as well he hadn't claimed to have feelings for her in return, at least, that's what she convinced herself of as they returned to Whitetail and Nolan left her at her door with a deep kiss that stirred her up all over again. *Suppressed hormones and a need to sate my long overdue horniness. That's all it is.* That had to be the reason her dreams continued to wake her shivering and aching for more of his painful stimulation just hours after climaxing beneath him.

"I'm turning into an insatiable hussy," Mia grumbled, rolling out of bed an hour later than usual the next morning. As she moved, she discovered how sore she was in a new way, a good way, she decided. It had been a long time since a man had been inside her. Her lips curved as she padded into the bathroom, stripped and looked at herself in the mirror. Compared to Nolan, her ex had definitely been lacking in more than size.

Signs of the previous night's debauchery decorated her skin from the slight pink whisker burn along her neck and breasts to a small bruise dotting her right buttock. A thrill tickled her senses from the proof of Nolan's possession, the uncharacteristic desire to show off the markings startling her. He seemed to have tapped into a side of Mia she'd never known existed, a side she liked.

The sudden rap on her door had her reaching for a robe as she heard Dee call out, "Hey, Mia, open up. You can't still be sleeping."

"Even if I was," she announced upon opening the door, "I wouldn't be now. Why are you here so early?"

"Early? You were supposed to host coffee and donuts after

church with me this morning. I had to cover for you. Why… *holy shit*!" Grabbing the sides of her robe, Dee spread it open without embarrassment. "Oh, wow, girlfriend. I want details, every raunchy second."

"Stop that." Mia laughed, yanking her robe closed and tightening the belt before turning to the coffee maker. "I had sex. Isn't that what you and Trish have been pushing me to do?"

"Well, yeah, but give, woman. Who? And just how wild did it get to leave you looking so freaking satisfied?"

Whirling, Mia grinned ear to ear. "I do? Cool. Oh, and it was Chief MacGregor."

Dee thrust a fist into the air with a *whoop*. "So, the rumors are true. I *knew* it!"

"Not until last night and… holy hell, Dee, the man is… *good*," she sighed.

"With that body and those eyes, he had to be. Tell me," Dee insisted, taking the mug Mia set in front of her on the kitchen counter. "Are the rumors of him being into kink true?"

Mia almost burned herself when her hand jerked, sloshing the hot coffee. She'd hoped to keep that part of her affair quiet. "Where'd you hear that?"

Her friend waved an airy hand, her face revealing unconcern over the trivial details. "I don't know. Maybe from Annie at the beauty shop. She's good friends with Daphne who went out with him a few times. Who knows and who cares?"

"I… look, yes, he's into a few things that are… new to me. But I don't want that bandied around. I mean it, or I won't tell you anything. I'm a businesswoman and need to keep up appearances if I intend to make a go of this place."

"I hear you. The bane of small towns and close-knit townsfolk. We get bored. You know you can trust me. Even though I'd hoped you were doing the nasty, I didn't let on this morning when people asked about you. I lied and said you weren't feeling well."

"Thanks, and I'm sorry I left you hanging. I was so tired when I got in, I forgot to set the alarm." She slid onto a stool next to Dee and sipped the coffee before telling her best friend what she wanted to know.

"Oh, wow, just… wow," Dee sighed, fanning herself. "It really was… I mean, you honestly *liked*… when he… I mean, even when he…"

"Yes, it really was, and yes, I honestly liked it, even when he…" Mia paused, wiggled her brows and grinned.

Shaking her head, Dee murmured, "If I wasn't so frigging happy with Bob, I'd hate you right now."

"I'm glad you are and that you don't. Now, go away. I have work to do."

Chapter 7

Mia emptied another bag of potting soil in Clifton Birmingham's garden along the side of his sprawling ranch house. Picking up her rake, she smoothed out the rich, dark earth around each Red Yucca plant until it lay evenly dispersed. The tall, red-bloomed flower stalks would do well along this side and would require little in the way of maintenance. Like they had been doing for the past two weeks, her thoughts strayed to Nolan. *I'm having an affair.* She still couldn't wrap her mind around that fact, or reconcile with the way she continued to respond to his every command, to both his painful and soothing touches with equal fervor and each time he took her. Whenever the sensations threatened to overwhelm her, or her chest grew tight and warm from a glance or a few words, she reminded herself she didn't like him.

"He's arrogant, bossy, irritating and… sexy as hell." Leaning her forehead on the top of the rake handle, she tried to get her act together and her mind back on the job. As much as she enjoyed wallowing in lust with the town's police chief, and yes, the envious looks that came their way whenever they were seen together by an eligible resident, or ineligible, she couldn't let it interfere with her work.

As soon as she closed at 2:00, she'd driven out here with two hours' worth of planting to accomplish and didn't have time to get distracted. Not by the way Nolan had strapped her down on the spanking bench in his playroom last night and fucked her from behind after inserting a butt plug and applying his belt four times across her cheeks, or the way she'd gone off like a firecracker. And not by his focused attention on her when he took her for a prime rib dinner at the steakhouse despite the obvious flirtations of the hostess, their waitress and an ex-girlfriend who'd insisted on stopping by their table and keeping her well-manicured hand on his shoulder the entire ten minutes she'd babbled on. And that was just two of the ten evenings they'd spent together in the last seventeen days.

After picking up the empty bags and her tools, she strolled toward the front of the house where she'd parked in the circle drive, wondering if she should continue to let this odd but satisfying relationship wear itself out or if she should worry about where it might, or might not lead. She wasn't in the market for another husband, and even if her interest in going that route were piqued again, it certainly wouldn't be with a man she didn't like, let alone love. Yet, every time she imagined doing the same things with someone else that Nolan had coerced her into, she turned cold.

No, best to let this relationship run its course; it had to burn out sooner or later. The hidden slutty side of her she'd never known she possessed would slither away soon—once, she was convinced, she'd made up for lost time and all those less than satisfying nights with Peter.

Striding toward her truck, Mia noticed a hedge of evergreen shrubs in need of pruning. She may as well earn brownie points with her best customer by taking care of it while she was here even though that row of greenery wasn't one she'd planted.

Tossing her things in the back of the truck, she realized she hadn't brought pruning shears. Thinking she might find one in the gardening shed she'd seen behind the large horse barn that housed Clifton's prized thoroughbreds, she set off across the lawn. In her opinion, it was an odd location for the shed, but even stranger was finding the door locked. Disappointed, she pivoted to return to the truck and stopped cold when she came face to face with the same creepy man she'd danced with at the Raging Bull and then seen leaving the seedier dive, County Line, with Barry a few weeks ago.

"What the hell are you doing snooping around back here?" he growled, his menacing tone matching the cold look in his black eyes.

Surprise sent her stumbling back a step as she stuttered, "I-I'm not snooping. I thought I'd find a pair of pruning shears in the shed."

"Isn't it your job to bring the tools you need?" he sneered, leaning with aggressive intent toward her.

Two other younger men came around the corner, and Mia breathed a sigh of relief when she recognized them as hands who tended the horses. Both had been courteous and friendly to her before and their presence helped to ease back the fear this man's sudden, threatening appearance instigated. Refusing to let the jerk intimidate her further, even if he did scare her, she looked him in the eye and stated, "I answer to Mr. Birmingham, not you. Step aside, please. I'm done here."

He saw the other two men and moved out of her way, but his ominous scowl never slipped as he said, "There are no gardening tools in this shed. Mr. Birmingham keeps veterinary supplies inside that could get stolen, so there's no need for you to come back here again."

Ignoring that comment, Mia rushed by him, waved to the two younger guys and breathed easier when she reached her truck just as Clifton emerged from the house. His gaze swung from her to the jerk who'd followed her, and he frowned in displeasure at whatever he saw on his employee's face. At least she wasn't the only one put off by the guy's behavior.

"Sanchez. Aren't you supposed to be working in the tack room?" Clifton asked.

"I heard your gardener here trying to get into the shed. Thought I'd best let her know you keep the ketamine under lock and key. Wouldn't want the kids working here thinking to have a little fun with that popular drug."

Mia didn't understand the humor lacing the creep's tone but was ready to be done with the man. "Sorry, Clifton. I forgot my shears and went looking for a pair. I'll tend your evergreen hedge next time I come out, or have the guys do it. Do you want to see what I did this afternoon?"

Clifton jogged down the steps, a smile softening his craggy features. "I just looked out there. Good work, as usual." He reached over and squeezed her shoulder as he instructed above her head, "Get back to work, Sanchez."

A cold shiver rippled under Mia's skin at Sanchez's thundercloud expression before he turned away and she wondered why Clifton put up with such blatant rudeness from an employee. Right or wrong to feel this way, the man's looks turned her stomach into a greasy knot of dread she couldn't ignore.

Clifton waited until Sanchez was out of earshot before his gaze turned apologetic. "I'm sorry if he was rude to you. Since rumor has it you're close to our new police chief, I'm sure MacGregor's mentioned the recent drug problem that's plagued the surrounding counties. I can't be too careful when I keep a strong anesthetic on site."

She hadn't heard about the recent drug traffic from Nolan, but news of a young overdose victim had been circulating around Whitetail, and being the mother of two boys the same age, she understood why Clifton kept the drugs locked up. But she still didn't appreciate Sanchez's aggressive, rude behavior, and worried anew about seeing him with Barry, despite her employee's explanation they'd just been leaving the bar at the same time. Something about the man screamed trouble and gave her the willies.

"No, I understand. We should be getting the last of your order with the fall plants in next week and finish your landscaping the following week. I'll talk to you then." Mia slid behind the wheel, anxious to get going.

Clifton nodded and shut the door for her. "Sounds good."

With a wave, she pulled away without glancing back. She didn't know why she thought she'd just dodged a bullet, but the jittery nerves hopping around inside her insisted she had. Shaking her head at her overblown response to an upsetting encounter, she tried to put the incident out of her mind as she reached the nursery, her thoughts shifting to Clifton's comment about the rumors of her and Nolan's affair. Before the divorce and her recent discovery of all she'd been missing out on, being the subject of such gossip would have appalled her. Now, as she spotted Nolan pulling in behind her, a giddy sense of excitement filled her at being linked with the town's bad boy turned chief law enforcer.

Watching him unfold his tall frame from the vehicle, tip his Stetson lower and saunter toward her with that loose-limbed stride that set her heart racing, was it any wonder Mia ended up agreeing to his terms? All of a sudden, she wanted him with an undeniable fervor, her pussy swelling from the way his cobalt gaze swept her sweat-streaked, dirt-smudged legs and arms and lit with pleasure despite her disheveled appearance. She needed a quick shower and then a round of fast, hot sweaty sex. God, she really had turned into a hussy.

"ARE YOU DONE FOR THE DAY?" Nolan hauled Mia against

him, the dirt smudge on her face a sign she'd been working.

"Yes, thank goodness." She leaned against him with a sigh, a rare gesture on her part and one that hinted her day had not gone well.

"C'mon. I picked up fried chicken. Let's go inside and you can tell me what you're not happy about."

She pulled back with a frown then turned away to mutter, "How do you do that?"

Grabbing the takeout box off the car seat, he asked, "Do what?" while taking her hand with his free one.

"Nothing. That smells good. The diner?"

"I couldn't pass up fried chicken Wednesday. Bridget said to tell you hello. She was there with her family." He released her hand to take the key from her at the top of the stairs.

"Don't you love the perks of small-town living?" she returned, her face reflecting dry amusement at them being linked together. He couldn't tell if that pleased her or not.

"Doesn't bother me. *I* happen to like *you*."

She flushed but instead of responding to that statement, said, "I need to take a quick shower. There's a pitcher of sun tea in the refrigerator."

Setting the chicken down on the kitchen counter, he eyed her with his best Dom look. "I like you disheveled and sweaty. Now, tell me what upset you today."

Placing her hands on her hips, Mia glared at him from the other side of the counter. "I agreed to let you call the shots for sex, Nolan. That doesn't mean revealing my every thought."

Annoyance tightened his gut as he returned her glare. He had no complaints about her willingness to submit to his sexual demands; in fact, her eager acceptance of everything he'd introduced her to and the way she responded so beautifully to his commands continued to both surprise and please him. What he found difficult to accept was her constant refusal to share any other part of herself. The more time he spent with her, the more he wanted, which was something he hadn't planned on or been aiming for. Unlike her, however, he was open to expanding their relationship beyond just a sexual one.

It took Nolan only a moment to decide to use her willingness to indulge the one aspect of their relationship to push for more. As he came around the counter, she must have read the intent on his face because she held up a hand and took a step back to ward off his approach. As if either would deter him.

"Oh, no." She shook her head but the gleam of interest in her green eyes said yes. "I told you I need to shower."

"I know." She turned to flee down the hall, but he moved faster and pinned her against the wall with the press of his body. With one hand sliding around to the front of her shorts, he whispered in her ear, "You can't shower dressed, now can you?"

A low groan spilled out of her mouth before she replied with a catch in her voice, "I guess not."

"You know, sweetheart." Nolan shoved her shorts down and then whipped her tee shirt over her head. "I can't be an effective Dom if you're not open with me." Her bra came off next and he filled his hands with the soft fullness of her breasts. "If something occurred to upset you and then I did something to trigger that memory, that could prove detrimental to us both." He tweaked her nipples before sliding his palms down her quivering abdomen until he reached her thighs. Cupping the inside of each, he pushed, urging them apart. "So, when I ask about your day, or inquire about what seems to be bothering you, it *is* part of our sexual relationship, and I don't appreciate your attitude."

"Well, how was I… *oh*!" His swat on her right buttock cut off her excuse with a gasp.

"You're supposed to trust me, that's how you should've known." He smacked her left cheek and then speared her damp pussy with two fingers while fishing a condom out of his pocket with his other hand. "If you don't know it by now, let me tell you. You can trust me with all of you, not just your body. I'm not your ex." Releasing his cock, he realized that last point pissed him off most. She continued to let Peter's betrayal color her view of all men and relationships.

"I know that. You're nothing like him." He drove into her slick channel, wanting more than the words from her. "*Oh, God.* I... I can't think straight... let alone talk... when you're... doing... that!"

Nolan lifted her hands and placed them flat against the wall before cupping her full breasts again as he withdrew. "Good. Don't think." He thrust back inside her, deep enough to bump against her womb. "Just feel and tell me what happened."

"What? Now?" Mia turned her head to stare at him in disbelief.

Pulling back by slow degrees, Nolan made sure to rasp over her clit before the only part of his shaft left inside her was his cockhead. "Now, Mia." Grabbing her nipples between his thumbs and forefingers, he pinched until she blanched.

"Fine," she huffed. "I had an... unpleasant encounter with one of Clifton Birmingham's employees. It left me... unsettled. That's all there is to it."

He would pull the man's name out of her later. First, he would reward her for her honesty. Releasing her nubs, he strummed over them with his thumbs as he surged back inside her. "Thank you. That wasn't so difficult, was it?"

"Just..." Her voice trailed off as he slid his hands down her sides to grasp her hips and yank them out further.

"Just what? Fuck you? Like this?" Holding her hips still, he plummeted into her convulsing depths with steady strokes, the first ripples of her climax washing over his cock within seconds. "That's it, Mia," he rasped. "Come all over me. Show me how much you want this, want me." He bent his head to her neck and bit.

"*Yes,*" she whimpered right before her cry of release shattered his control.

MIA OPENED the bathroom door to the wonderful aroma of fried chicken stirring her hunger. She'd taken her time in the shower, not sure how she felt about Nolan's tactics to get her to talk to him about matters she considered private and that had nothing to do with their relationship. His explanation made sense, once she thought about it, but his tactics rankled as much as her easy compliance. The deep wound caused by Peter's betrayal still pained her, and she'd vowed long ago never to give a man access to her inner thoughts and feelings again. The callous way her ex had thrown both in her face along with his young girlfriend was embedded in her mind, and even though she no longer loved him, his cruel words still held the power to hurt.

Her buttocks still tingled from those two hard swats and her sheath continued to pulse from Nolan's rough possession. It was always that way, and her responses to his handling didn't appear to be dwindling as she'd first assumed they would. Still, she'd been celibate for a long time and unfulfilled for even longer, although she hadn't realized that at the time. Nolan proved that dismal fact the first time he bent her over and swatted her butt. The memory almost made her giggle like a schoolgirl. The pleasure to be gained from an adult, bare-bottomed spanking continued to astound her.

Walking into the kitchen, she eyed the way he set her small table along with the chicken, coleslaw and potato salad. "I'm starving but if I eat all of that I'll gain ten pounds."

Nolan looked her over with a critical eye before saying, "You hold your weight just fine. I like the look of you, and the feel of you. Since we're not seeing anyone else while we're together, that's all that matters."

"We're not?" Mia took a seat, his statement pleasing her on a level she wasn't prepared for. That plane where she might start to care more than she planned for, more than was wise.

"No, we're not." He piled her plate with food but watched her closely as he asked, "Do you have a problem with that?"

"No, not at all. It's just… I'm surprised by your willingness to remain monogamous given the rumors I've heard about you."

"Don't believe everything you hear."

"I usually don't." She took a bite of potatoes before she couldn't help mentioning his numerous flower orders. "The number of plants and arrangements you've ordered from me lend credence to the gossip, don't you agree?"

His lips quirked with amusement she didn't understand. "You would think so, wouldn't you? To be clear, I've never slept with anyone from Whitetail whom I took out except you."

That didn't explain the flowers, but Mia was uncomfortable with the conversation and the rush of warm relief his confession produced. She shrugged, hoping to convey an indifference she didn't feel. "If you say so."

"I do, and since you can trust me, you can believe that. Since my return, I've limited sex to the club. Given my job and status, I thought that best for now. Speaking of which, I'm scheduled to put time in as monitor Saturday night. Are you ready for another visit?"

If the way her body just sped into heated overdrive were anything to go by, Mia figured the answer would be an emphatic yes. Knowing what to expect seemed to ease any misgivings she still harbored for the as yet unknown aspects of his kinks. "Sure, I'll go."

He nodded as if expecting that reply. "Friday night I'm headed back to the County Line since no one else is available to stake it out that night. Want to keep me company?"

"Do you honestly believe drugs are coming through someone in Whitetail?" Mia couldn't think of a single person who would do such a thing.

"I don't want to, but border patrol and the Feds are convinced of it. If I can catch a deal going down, it would give me someone to interrogate, which is more than we have now, and the sleazier bars are the most likely places for a meet."

She didn't care to return to that particular dive, but when she imagined Nolan there alone, maybe dancing with another woman to mingle closer with the other patrons, she cared even less for that possibility. "Sure, I'll go and even help you look for the bad guys."

"You'll stay out of it, I mean it, Mia. You don't know how to observe others unnoticed but the people who deal drugs for a living can. You'll make a good cover just by being with me."

He stared at her with his most stern Dom look, the one she'd learned was impossible to argue with. "Fine. I'll be your arm candy. That'll be a first for me."

"As long as you know you're more than that, you can portray yourself however you want."

CLIFTON HUNTED down Sanchez after he'd had time to cool off. He found him in the tack room, where he should have stayed when Mia Reynolds went looking for pruning shears. He was surrounded by imbeciles and was getting damned tired of it.

"What the hell did you think you were doing?" he demanded as he shut the small room's door behind him and placed his fists on his hips. He'd come too far to let this moron take him down or put a crimp in his lucrative side dealings.

Sanchez flicked him a disdainful sneer and kept tanning the saddle lying over a sawhorse. "You'd have preferred I let her keep snooping?"

"She wasn't snooping and wasn't suspicious of anything until you tried scaring her off. Why didn't you just wave a red flag in front of her or, better yet, unlock the damn shed and invite her inside?" *Fucking moron.*

"First off, *boss*," he drawled in sarcasm, "I didn't know what she was doing or looking for when I came out of the barn and saw her. But I did recall she saw me leaving the County Line the same time as one of her employees. If any of our guys are made there, it won't take her long to remember me."

Clifton shook his head in disgust. "And, so what? You've sworn you've covered your tracks and there's nothing to lead you to me, or either of us to our sideline. Again, all you had to do was let it go. Think you can manage to do that from now on?"

"I can manage," he ground out, his hands tightening on the leather and his eyes going dark with anger.

Unfazed, Clifton pivoted and opened the door while delivering a parting shot. "See that you do." With Mia now hooked up with their new police chief, it would be wise to make some quick changes. The only problem with that was the changes needed weren't easy to make and would take considerable time and effort. With his connection refusing to do anything about the tainted drugs slipping in with the pure stuff, he needed to consider getting out.

The problem with that was people who left this organization often ended up dead or never heard from again.

"NO FUCKING WAY, CAMPBELL." Nolan shoved back from his desk and, holding the phone to his ear, listened to his former boss while slamming the door shut for both privacy and anger release. "Your man is wrong," he bit out as he strode over to the window that looked out upon the city park. Preparations were already underway for the annual Fourth of July citywide picnic, an event he'd planned to attend with Mia. Hell, everything he wanted to do he wanted to do with her.

"Look, Chuck. I know Mia Reynolds and I'm telling you she is not involved, and I don't give a rat's ass what intel your man has passed on. If drugs are being funneled through the state with landscaping orders, she is one owner who knows nothing about it." A cold knot of dread took up residence in his gut despite his unequivocal belief in what he just said. Mia's naïve innocence sometimes bordered on ridiculous given her age and the fact she'd been married for almost twenty years. But that was the part of her charm that had first drawn him and continued to please him. He never tired of seeing the flash of stunned disbelief in her eyes when he tormented her into orgasm.

Chuck Campbell's frustrated sigh echoed through the phone. "Look, Nolan, you asked for something to go by and I'm giving it to you. My guy said to check it out, and that's what we're going to do. If you know the woman that well, how hard can it be for you to visit her nursery and look around, maybe catch wind of when the next shipment's due to arrive?"

"You want me to spy on her?"

"I want you to do your job," Chuck retorted. "If you need a reminder of what we're up against, pull out the death photos of the last victim of these drugs. I'll be in touch."

Nolan tossed the phone on his desk without glancing back. Chuck didn't realize the betrayal he was asking of him. Mia still struggled with what her ex put her through. How could he betray her trust also? He'd pursued her and started this affair for the sole purpose of giving her the chance to explore everything he'd suspected she yearned for. And yes, the macho side of him desired to erase the pain of her husband's deception from her pretty green eyes. But the surprising depth of his need to know what had occurred to upset her the other day revealed his feelings were now irrevocably involved, and he was okay with that.

"What a cluster fuck," he mumbled, running a hand through his hair in indecision. Chuck was right, he had a job to do, which included getting answers for a grieving family. He prayed Mia never got wind of his involvement once he proved neither she nor her business were being used as a stopping post for the illegal drug route cutting through the state.

Chapter 8

Mia glanced askance at Nolan as they walked up to the County Line entrance. Like last time, the crowded parking lot hinted at the number of people inside, with the noise pouring out when he held open the door just as deafening. For the first time since she'd agreed to this affair, he seemed preoccupied with something other than her when they were together. She hadn't realized how much she'd relished his undivided attention until now, when she no longer had it. Stepping inside, she found herself hoping it was his job, the drug case and recent overdose that were preying on his mind tonight and not dissatisfaction with her. She wasn't ready for this to end yet.

Tugging on her hand, he nodded toward a vacant corner table. "Let's grab that one."

Mia nodded, refusing to shout over the raucous din. Winding their way through the throng of jostling bodies, she sank onto the chair he held for her with a sigh. She didn't want to be here. The two previous times she'd ventured out to the bars, she'd had her friends and a need to prove to herself she could move on from the end of her marriage to bolster her enthusiasm. Tonight, it didn't take long for her to discover she'd rather spend the evening alone with Nolan, or at his club in Albuquerque. Ever since he mentioned making a return trip, it was all she could think about.

Lifting a finger to catch the waitress's attention, he leaned over and spoke close to her ear to be heard. "What do you want to drink?"

His warm breath blew down her neck and set up goosebumps along her arms, a nice distraction from the crowd. "Beer is fine, anything light."

Nodding, he placed their order and then pointed across the room. "Look who's here."

Curious about the displeasure reflected on his face, Mia glanced that way and spotted Barry, Donny and Drew seated at the bar. While she wished the kids would entertain themselves at a more reputable establishment, they were of legal age to be in here and served alcohol. "After seeing Barry here last time, I spoke with him about maybe going somewhere less risky. I guess he blew off my suggestion."

"Looks like."

She didn't understand the tight set to his mouth until she remembered the overdose victim had been their age. Putting a hand on his rigid forearm, she tried to reassure him. "They're good kids, Nolan. I've encountered no trouble from them."

"Weren't you complaining about Barry the other day?"

"Only his habitual tardiness and missed days." She shrugged, trying to make light of it and didn't mention Barry's insolent looks. It wasn't the first time she'd dealt with a cocky, attitude-riddled teenager.

"Let's hope you're right. Come on."

Rising, Nolan led her onto the dance floor for a slow number and her silent objections to the crowd melted away when he pulled her close. It had been like that each time he'd nudged another inch past her defenses, from coping with her ex to succumbing to his sexual demands and her responses. If he was near and the one giving the orders, she handled both her ex and her unexpected, wayward libido much better. She liked that perk about their relationship. She also liked the way he danced, the feel of his muscled legs moving against hers, her breasts pressed against his wide chest, the tight clasp of his arms and hands and the gleam of lust shining in his blue eyes as he looked down at her. Without his hat, the steely grey strands that framed his forehead and emphasized the inky darkness of the rest of his hair were more noticeable. She liked… him.

Mia stumbled from that revelation, her eyes flying up to Nolan's face and then shifting away from his sharp, assessing gaze. She remembered all too well how adeptly he'd extracted the incident at Clifton's from her. He touched her, and she turned to putty. It had been that way since he'd pulled her over after leaving this same bar a few short weeks ago and now look at her. She'd grown to *like* the man.

"What's wrong?" Nolan asked, tightening his arms around her. "And look at me when you answer."

Shit. Irritation replaced the unease that admission stirred up. Whipping her gaze back up to his, she schooled her features to bland coolness. "I missed a step. The crowd and noise are bothering me."

Mia couldn't tell if he believed her when he nodded and said, "We'll leave soon then. Let's finish our drinks."

"I'll meet you at the table. I want to visit the restroom first." Slipping out of his arms, she didn't look at him again as she waded through the gyrating bodies on the dance floor and padded down the short hall leading to the bathrooms. Gripping the edge of the sink, she took a deep breath, trying to calm her racing pulse. She liked him, so what? It didn't have to mean anything more than that, in fact, that was a good thing. After all, what did it say about her she'd started an affair with a man she didn't like? The thing that shook her was how fast the tables had turned. That's what scared Mia, because if like came that fast, that easy, love might too, and that's something she'd vowed never to open herself up for again.

"He's not even my type," she muttered, straightening. That reminder made her feel better. There was no way she could feel a stronger emotion for someone who was the complete opposite of… whom? Peter was the only man she'd been with before Nolan, as pathetic as that was. She'd fallen for him so hard, so fast, she'd never questioned whether he was the man for her, and never had anyone to compare him with. When she'd ended up pregnant and scared, she'd jumped at the chance to marry fast and never looked back until the day Peter asked for a divorce.

Mia ran her fingers through her hair, wishing Nolan would quit demanding she leave it loose when they were together. A few more weeks, she insisted. By then, surely whatever this was would have fizzled out and she could go back to concentrating on her business and enjoying evenings out with friends.

She left the bathroom trying to make up excuses for the pang that last thought wrought and jolted unprepared when she caught sight of that creep Sanchez again, this time heading for the bar. He spotted her at the same time, stopped, scowled and pivoted, as if he didn't want to be anywhere near her, which worked for her. The boys remained glued to their barstools, so she was glad Sanchez opted for a seat away from them. A hard hand wrapped around her arm, startling her until she looked up into Nolan's dark face.

With a tilt of his head, he asked, "Is everything okay?"

For once, Mia was grateful for the way he kept a close eye on her, but she didn't want to start anything between him and Clifton's employee. "Yes. It's just… some of these people give me the willies, if you know what I mean." The shiver he noticed wasn't feigned or exaggerated, but thankfully he didn't press her on it.

"Yeah, I know what you mean. Always trust your instincts, sweetheart. I'm ready, if you are."

"I am. And, Chief? If I had trusted my instincts with you, we wouldn't be having an affair."

NOLAN TURNED into Greenleaf Nursery Saturday morning and saw Mia already boasted a booming Saturday business. He'd seen one of the men on his list of those to watch again last night, the same man who had his hands all over Mia at the Raging Bull a few weeks ago, but still nothing he could bring him in for. He didn't show up on his searches through mug shots, but that meant nothing.

Shoving aside the bitter taste of what he was here to do, he slid out of his cruiser and glanced in the window of the floral shop, spotting Mia behind the counter wearing a frown as she worked on the computer. As tempted as he was to find out the reason for her irritation and dispel her of it, he walked into the yard instead. Under the guise of shopping for outdoor plants, he took his time strolling up and down the rows of native foliage, visiting with townsfolk he knew while eyeing every corner of the yard for a possible nook to hide and transfer anything illegal coming in with the rest of the plants. Only Drew and Donny were around to help customers, which might account for the displeasure he'd seen on Mia's face.

The greenhouse doors were open, and he stepped inside the humid heat of the condensed greenery, seeing how easy it would be for someone to slip cannabis plants among the rest of the smaller shrubbery, but no obvious route for the tainted cocaine powder to come through. From his years with the DEA, he'd learned how creative drug smugglers could get, and putting false bottoms on shipping containers such as wood crates or decorative items such as ceramic vases wasn't unheard of. But without upending those items scattered around the lot, he couldn't do anything without a warrant and drawing a lot of questions and suspicions.

And if it came down to getting a warrant, that meant he had proof that could send Mia to prison. *Fuck.* No way would he believe her capable of being involved in the drug trade, or anything else illegal. Other than her penchant for getting tickets, she was the most strait-laced, law-abiding person he knew.

As much as it went against everything he felt for Mia, Nolan took the time to peruse the row of large ceramic planters lined up along the outside of the shop, tipping a few sideways as if inspecting them for purchase. She had yet to venture out—he didn't even know if she knew he was here—but one of the college kids approached him with a smile.

"Hey, Chief. Can I help you find something?"

"Drew, right?" With his red hair and freckles, he still looked more like a high schooler than a second-year college student.

"Right." With a wave of his arm, Drew offered, "These will hold just about any of our perennials and make it easy to switch them out every year."

"That's just what I was thinking," Nolan lied. "I'm headed in to talk to your boss. I'll let her help me choose one, but thanks for your help."

"Anytime, Chief."

Feeling the kid's eyes on him, Nolan opened the shop's side door, hating his job for the first time since accepting this new position. Mia and Trish both glanced up as the bell tolled over the door and he stepped inside. Trish ceased spraying the row of small indoor plants in front of her to wave and greet him.

"Hey, Chief MacGregor. How are you?"

"Good, Trish. Thanks." One other woman was shopping along the shelves holding small garden ceramics in the form of whimsical creations as he crossed over to the counter.

"Good morning, Mia. What has you frowning on such a

pleasant day?" He cocked his head, tipping his hat back to gaze upon her disgruntled features.

"A delay in a shipment, Barry calling in sick again and an outbreak of aphids." She nodded toward Trish. "Easy enough to get under control with spraying, but an added chore I don't need today. What brings you in?"

"I wanted to see you, let you know I'll pick you up at seven." It took effort, but he managed to keep from smiling when she flushed and cast a quick glance toward Trish and her customer before replying in a hushed undertone.

"Yes, I told you last night I'll be ready."

"Just making sure. Relax. Everyone already knows we're seeing each other," he drawled. But, just to rile her further and see that flash of irritation cross her face that always stirred his cock, he leaned across the counter, reached behind her head, cupped her nape and drew her forward. Before she could protest, he kissed her hard and fast and then slid his mouth to her ear and whispered, "I want you bare of pubic hair tonight. Don't disappoint me or you won't sit for a week." He brushed his knuckles under her chin as he pulled back, not surprised to see her eyes widen with both shock and arousal. "Later, sweetheart."

"DAMN MAN IS ALWAYS CROWDING ME," Mia mumbled as Nolan strode out, her mind whirling around his latest dictate, and the embarrassing but erotic possibilities it posed. Exposing that sensitive flesh to his gaze would mortify her, but she shuddered imagining how the calloused pads of his fingers would feel, or his lips or tongue…

"Honey, that man can crowd me anywhere, anytime," Mrs. Anders commented with a smile as she set two garden gnomes on the counter for her to ring up.

"Me too," Trish tossed out. "If you're ever dumb enough to let him go, I get dibs!"

Flustered, sure her face had turned as red as the carnations she stocked for Valentines' Day, Mia shook her head and rang up the purchases, keeping her mouth shut. Would she ever stop reacting so strongly to Nolan and the things he wanted from her? Not only was she still struggling to accept the way he could turn her into a limp noodle with just a look or kiss no matter where they were, and with her recent change of heart from dislike to like for the arrogant, bossy police chief, but she couldn't keep from worrying about his distracted mood last night and even this morning. She'd seen him pull up and watched through the windows as he'd looked around while conversing with some of her other customers, but she'd noticed his preoccupation with something else, just like last night. Of that she was sure. Unlike the way he'd insisted and pushed for her to reveal her every thought, she couldn't get up the nerve to ask him what was wrong, and she cared more than she should—or was wise—about his feelings.

"What do you and our chief have planned tonight? And, can I watch?" Trish teased when Mrs. Anders left, and they were alone in the shop.

A grin tugged at Mia's lips. Thinking about returning to the mansion, she found amusement in how close Trish was to what went on there. "We're going to Albuquerque, and no, you can't watch."

"Party pooper. I guess I must grab someone else to hang with at the Raging Bull."

"Don't go alone," she cautioned the younger girl. "And be careful. You've heard the gossip about drugs as well as I."

"Yes, Mom," Trish teased.

Giving her a mock frown, Mia said, "Mind the store. I'll be outside, lecturing Drew and Donny next."

As it turned out, the guys were working hard and making

sales, so she never got the chance to hint they should stay clear of places like the County Line, at least until the authorities put a stop to the tainted drugs going around. By the time 5:00 rolled around, she was eager to get ready to go out with Nolan and only took time to praise them for their hard work.

"Hey, you two," she said, strolling over to where Drew was sweeping the walk while Donny stacked empty crates. "You did a great job today, and I appreciate you picking up the pace due to Barry's slack. If he keeps this up, he may leave me with no choice but to let him go. I can't expect you to continue to carry the load for three."

Donny brushed his hands off, replying, "Don't worry, Ms. Reynolds. After we lay into him tonight, he'll think twice before continuing to party on a work night after we return to the dorm from clubbing, like he did last night." His eyes reflected the same aggravation Mia felt with Barry.

"We're both planning on giving him a piece of our minds," Drew put in. "You and the chief sure are getting tight. That's cool."

Recognizing the ploy to change the subject, she drawled, "Glad you approve. Take off, you two. I can finish this up." They didn't argue and by the time she closed down and trotted upstairs to her apartment, she had less than an hour before Nolan returned.

MIA HOPED Nolan couldn't sense her nervous excitement as he escorted her inside the club mansion a few hours later. She'd barely made it through the process of shaving an area she'd never imagined baring before hooking up with him and then sitting through dinner without revealing her reaction every time the soft silk of her panties brushed over that sensitive, newly exposed skin. Each innocent move set off sparks of heat tingling over her labia and spreading up her core. She'd debated over whether to go for the spanking and ignore his instruction to shave. With the punishment, she'd known what her response to his hand on her butt would be, so she'd chosen the new and unknown. Who knew how much longer she would have to explore these things? She certainly couldn't picture herself doing what she'd done with Nolan with anyone else.

Now, as she stepped inside the dim foyer, her panties so damp they stuck to her flesh, the need throbbing between her legs begged to be assuaged.

"Are you sure everything is okay?" Nolan asked her for the fourth time since picking her up.

"Yes," she returned, sending him a disgruntled look. "But had I known the results of obeying your order to… shave for tonight, I think I would have risked the punishment."

"That wouldn't have gotten you out of it, just delayed it. Only, after I enjoyed the fun of walloping on your delectable ass, I would have enjoyed the pleasure of seeing to the chore myself."

Mia halted and gaped at him, his serious tone and look telling her he meant it. It had been embarrassing enough when she'd attended to the matter herself, she couldn't imagine getting through it with him doing the deed. "Sometimes, I don't know how to react to you, or what to say."

"I know. That's what makes you so much fun. You look good wearing shorter dresses. Do it more often."

She bristled at that succinct command but the warm glow his approving, heated gaze conjured up overrode her irritation. He'd surprised her by showing up with the body molding sheath that fell just shy of exposing her butt with each step, and insisted she wear it tonight. The summer green complemented her tanned arms and legs, but she wasn't comfortable with the snug fit. She hadn't been a skinny teen and carried even more weight now. Although, she had to admit Nolan didn't seem to mind her softer, fuller figure.

"You're the only one who seems to appreciate my… extra curves."

"I'm the only one who matters, at least right now. There's Master Blake, one of my partners in this place. Remember to be respectful, to me and others," he cautioned as he placed a hand on her lower back and urged her into the large gathering room where several people already mingled.

In this environment, Nolan was right, his opinion was the only one Mia cared about. The other people were nice, but Master Blake's appreciative gaze and friendly greeting didn't make her insides do funny things the way Nolan's did. Nor did anyone else's.

"It's nice to meet you… Sir." The title came easier than she'd thought, and she put it down to the ego boost his look gave her even though she didn't respond to the favorable approval in his blue eyes the way she did to Nolan's cobalt gaze.

"It's nice to see Master Nolan bring a guest, Mia. Welcome to the club."

"Master Nolan!"

Mia released Master Blake's hand and turned toward the *young* and very *slender* girl clutching Nolan's arm and staring up at him with an excited, animated expression. Her heart rolled over and her abdomen tightened as she sidled closer to his side, the urge to pry the girl's hand off his arm and then claw her eyes out one she'd never experience toward another person in her life. She couldn't recall one time when she'd felt as possessive over Peter as she did now, over Nolan… Master Nolan.

"Angie." Nolan kissed the fawning girl's cheek then gently shifted his arm out from under her grip.

"Do you have someone for your cupping demonstration yet? If not, I'd *love* to volunteer." Angie bounced on bare toes, setting her perky breasts covered only by a sheer, baby doll nightie to swaying.

"Cupping?" Mia asked. She had heard of the ancient

Chinese form of alternative medicine but knew nothing else about the practice. She did know she didn't care for the gleam in Angie's eyes as she looked at Nolan.

Nolan blew out a frustrated breath and ran a hand through his hair, two sure signs he was uncomfortable about something. "I promised to demonstrate the practice and how someone can apply it to enhance a scene. You can watch it from the viewing window into the demonstration room upstairs." He squeezed the hand he hadn't released since ushering her inside.

Before Mia could think it through, she blurted, "I'll do it." Regardless of the public exposure she wasn't comfortable with, there was no way she wanted to watch his hands all over Angie, bringing the young girl to orgasm.

Frowning, Nolan spoke to Angie and Master Blake when he stated, "Excuse me a minute, please," before ushering her over to a quiet corner. "You don't know what you're getting into, Mia. This scene will be very intense, not to mention it being conducted with public viewing. Why don't—"

"No, I want to do it." She injected a lightness to her tone as she asked, "How hard can it be?" He swore under his breath and she winced but stood her ground by turning stubborn. "I want to do this. You keep telling me I have a lot to learn. I can't do that by standing on the sidelines."

NOLAN WOULD TURN Mia down flat if he could swear that wasn't envy turning her eyes a shade greener, an emotion he wouldn't have appreciated coming from any other sub. From her, it was a step in the direction he wanted her to go in this relationship. If he turned her down, as he knew he should, she might consider him doing a scene with Angie a betrayal. Considering what her ex had put her through and his own deceit in checking out her nursery for drug deliveries, he couldn't do that to her.

"Fine, but once we're in the demonstration room, no balking at the last minute, or I swear I'll take a strap to you." He almost laughed when her nipples hardened under the thin, stretchy material of her dress.

"I won't," she insisted.

Nolan shook his head. "God help us both. Let me have a word with Master Blake and then we'll go upstairs." He left her with a small group before taking a minute to enlist Blake's assistance, letting him know he intended to move fast and keep it simple in deference to Mia's innocence. Fire cupping was most common in BDSM but could freak out an untried newbie. He knew what he was doing and had enough practice in the art to ensure her safety, which aided in his decision to let her participate.

The second floor room used to give presentations of different BDSM practices was set up with a padded bench, and items for cupping were stored in the wall cabinet along with an array of fun implements. Nolan could feel Mia's arm tremble as he ushered her inside and she spotted the way the bench faced the viewing pane. "Change your mind?" he asked, crossing his arms and tightening his jaw against the urge to order her to do just that. This had to be her decision.

Her shoulders squared, and her jaw locked in determination. "No." Cocking her head, she prodded, "You did say I could trust you, right?"

"Yes, but that doesn't mean I don't think you're still too new for this scene." Waving a hand toward her, he ordered, "Strip and hop on the bench."

Mia bit her lower lip, her eyes shifting from him to the window where several people already gathered in the adjoining room. Pink stained her cheeks, but she lowered the thin dress straps and shimmied out of it, keeping her face down once she stood before him clad in nothing but a pair of panties. Damp silk clung to the denuded shape of her labia and his fingers itched to touch that soft, plump flesh.

"Panties too." She flashed him a look of mild irritation and major consternation but kept quiet as she stepped out of the green underwear and laid them on top of her dress on the corner chair. Clasping her waist, he lifted her onto the bench, enjoying the way she gripped his forearms to steady herself. "You are a beautiful," he cupped one breast and strummed the nipple, "sexy woman, Mia." With a pinch to the rigid tip, he left her sitting there to rummage in the cabinet. Holding up a blindfold, he said, "Like at my house, you'll fare better if you concentrate on feeling instead of fretting over who is watching."

"I'm not fretting," she returned as he secured the black satin over her eyes. "I don't like people seeing me naked."

"I enjoy showing you off, and you like being naked in front of me." Nolan skimmed his fingers over the smooth skin of her glistening folds. "Your body doesn't lie." Turning her shoulders, he guided her to lie down on her stomach. "No talking during a demonstration unless you need to use one of the safewords. If you're unsure about continuing, say yellow. Save red for when you know you don't want me to keep going."

Master Blake slipped inside the room without a word as Nolan retrieved the oil. Speaking to his audience through the speakers, he began his lecture. "Relaxing your sub is paramount to ensuring a successful scene with cupping, especially with an inexperienced submissive." Noting the immediate stiffening of Mia's body as her brows lowered in a frown, he waved his hand over her tense back, swinging his gaze toward the viewers. "Starting with a massage will aid in easing any tension your sub feels about going forward. An experienced Dom can read his partner's body as easily as her face and knows which expression to go by." He flicked his fingers against her compressed lips, drawing Blake's grin.

Setting the oil down, Nolan kept his eyes on Mia's face

turned toward him as he and Blake, standing on opposite sides of the bench, drew the straps over her wrists. The second she realized there were two men, she jerked with a gasp and lifted her head.

"Nolan?"

Hearing the tremor of vulnerability behind the whisper of uncertainty, he leaned over her and taunted in a low voice, "Are you going to prove me right before I've even begun?"

Her mouth tightened, and she shook her head. "I'm fine with… it, if you are," she bit out.

"Sweetheart, you'll be more than fine with the extra hands by the time we're through." They strapped her ankles apart next and then Nolan oiled his hands before passing the bottle over to Blake with a nod.

Chapter 9

"Mia is new to our club, but brave enough to volunteer tonight. It's my job to reward her for her trust by ensuring she has a positive experience."

Mia shivered from Nolan's deep voice and succumbed to the pleasure of four hands kneading her shoulders, then down her back and legs before working their way back up to her buttocks. She stiffened at first and then moaned in pleasure as the two men squeezed her malleable globes with their talented fingers, digging in to her soft flesh and manipulating the tension right out of her. Her mind started to drift on a pleasant haze of comfort when one pair of hands left her body followed by the distinct sound and smell of a flame being lit. Before she could voice the objection clogging her throat with instant fear, a round glass object pressed on her butt, the heat inside the globe sucking up the air, drawing her flesh up inside, the tight sensation bordering on uncomfortable.

"The larger cups cover a bigger area, such as the buttocks. I can leave them on for up to ten minutes as the flame eats up the air inside the cup, drawing the flesh up with it before the alcohol-soaked wand burns itself out."

A low moan slid past her compressed lips when the massage continued around her 'cupped' buttock before Nolan slid a finger around the rim and pried the glass off. She honestly couldn't tell if the sudden rush of blood alleviated or added to the discomfort.

"The oil will help with keeping the bruising to a minimum as well as aids in adhering the cup to the skin and in removing it. Mia, you're doing well. Let's turn you over."

By the time they unstrapped her and flipped her over, she lay limp as a wet noodle and the spot on her buttock pulsed and itched, stirring her arousal, making it difficult to lie still as they re-bound her arms and legs. Despite the cool air wafting over the front of her body drawing goosebumps, heat washed over her face as she pictured her spread thighs and bare pussy left gaping for the audience.

Mia sucked in a deep breath and catapulted into sensory overload the minute those large, oil-slicked hands touched her again. The dual kneading of her breasts stripped away her unease over baring her round body in front of strangers, the simultaneous brush of thumbs over her nipples sending an arrow of heat down to her already aching core.

As they massaged their way down her quivering abdomen, her breath stalled in her throat. When they squeezed her inner thighs, their thumbs grazing her seam, her gasp echoed in the room. If she hadn't been restrained, Mia knew she would have gone flying off the bench from the sizzle that simple touch ignited along the delicate flesh of her denuded labia. She shook from the potent, stimulating impact of exposing sensitive nerve endings she'd never realized were there. Her breath released on a whoosh as they slid away from those throbbing tissues and, like magic, their slow massage down her legs lulled her further into complacency.

The low hum of arousal spread through her body, barely there, just enough to keep her warm when their hands would leave one area to travel to another. The other man kept quiet as

Nolan spoke more of cupping, the dos and don'ts of the practice she took little heed of. He'd convinced her she could trust him, and from the way her body was responding to yet another new experience, she had nothing to fear except maybe losing another piece of herself to the man she'd only just now come to like.

Nolan, she knew, stood on her left and she could sense him moving away even though the other man continued to massage a return trail up her leg. His touch felt different now that Nolan wasn't joining in. Even though his hands still eased the tension in her muscles as he rubbed over her hip and waist again, a chill racked her body and she turned her head in search of Nolan.

"Nolan?" A sharp slap on the inside of her thigh drew a startled cry, the familiar burn and throb of pain having its usual, speedy effect.

"That's Master Nolan, and I told you not to speak unless it's to issue a color. Is that what you are doing?" he asked from right above her.

How could he expect her to remember all those little rules now? "No, I'm… fine," she mumbled, careful not to risk another mortifying reprimand. Or was it the dampness she could feel pooling between her legs that embarrassed her?

His breath blew into her ear and his rough jaw scratched her cheek as he bent and whispered, "Good. I'd hate to have to stop before I've even begun. I'm proud of you, sweetheart."

Mia's heart executed that funny roll again and she turned her face enough to brush his mouth with hers. With her sight cut off, all of her other senses picked up the slack, making every sound louder, every touch more pronounced. Even the earthy male scent of him she'd always found appealing tickled her nose more than usual.

With a squeeze to her shoulder, he moved away, and she heard him pick up something before the strike of another flame produced another jolt of alarm. Before she could panic and cry red as she imagined him applying the device to more sensitive areas, the other man bent to her ear and she recognized Master Blake's voice.

"Master Nolan knows what he's doing. Relax, you're in good hands." He distracted her by cupping her breast and flicking her nipple, but she still heard Nolan's explanation.

"The idea behind cupping, whether through fire or pumping suction, is to bring additional blood flow, and thus sensation, to the area. The larger cups can also be used on the inner thighs."

Like he had on her cheek, he laid a round, glass object high on the inside of her thigh, the heat drawing up the air as well as the flesh close to her vulnerable crotch. Discomfort gave way to sharp, intense sensation several minutes later as he removed the cup and left the area feeling tight and achy, in a shockingly good way. Mia whimpered when he treated the inside of her opposite thigh to the same erotic torture, the throbbing of her taut flesh matching the area on her butt and spreading to her vagina. Master Blake continued to tease her nipples, stroking, pinching, twisting until the small buds pulsed in a similar fashion, just not as intense.

One finger traced over her labia and up her slit as Nolan embarrassed her further by pointing out the obvious. "You can already see the effect cupping has on my sub, and I haven't even gotten to her nipples and this pretty pussy yet."

Just imagining the heated cups drawing on such tender flesh zapped Mia with a lightning bolt of lust. Grateful for the blindfold, she waited with bated breath upon hearing the lighter again. A much smaller cup covered her right nipple and sucked onto the flesh surrounding it. She bit her lip against the drawing pressure then breathed a sigh of relief when multiple fingers kneaded her waist and on down to her tense thighs. By the time Nolan gently removed the cup from over her nipple, the nub was engorged and drawn into a tight, throbbing pinch.

Nolan moved to her other nipple while Blake continued the massage, sliding his hands over her oil-slick, sensitive body with expertise. Heat drew her left nipple up into the cup and reality faded as raw, sexual hunger invaded Mia's body and took command of her senses. The pounding of unfulfilled lust reverberated in her head, drowning out the drone of Nolan's voice.

With her nipples now so tender any touch would set her off, he placed another fired-up cup between her legs to pull on the most delicate and already aching part of her body. Mia didn't need to see her body to know how swollen her labia was when he removed the cup minutes later; didn't need a touch on the hypersensitive flesh to prove how primed she was to go off like a firecracker.

Nolan's voice drifted to her through the haze. "Swollen, beautiful and needy. I'd say my sub deserves a reward for being such a good participant tonight."

"For a newbie, she's a gem." Master Blake's compliment warmed her as much as Master Nolan's.

Without further warning, fingers grazed Mia's nipples and slid past her puffy folds to tickle her inflamed clit. One touch and an orgasm hit her with hard waves of gasping pleasure, sweeping through her body like a drenching, body-flinging tsunami.

MIA SPENT Sunday morning walking around on cloud nine. After awakening spooned with her back against Nolan's front, his cock pressing into her pussy from behind, she'd enjoyed starting the day with an orgasm followed by cooking breakfast for a man who made his appreciation known in delightful ways. The hint of caring in his tone during the previous night's demonstration affected her as much as his touch and the surreal experience, and she'd vowed to relish the pleasure of that rather than fret over where they might be headed with this affair. He'd left her place that morning with a promise to come by later, and that's as far ahead at a time as she wanted to go.

While the unbelievable sensations he'd wrought from her during the cupping demonstration still possessed the power to draw a shiver from just thinking about it, she still struggled with her willingness to put herself in such an exposed, vulnerable position because of an unexpected bout of envy. When agreeing to the terms of an affair with Nolan, Mia had known he was a sexually dominant man, but never dreamed she would crave that side of him as an addict would his next fix. Honesty forced her to admit she didn't know how she felt about that, which made it best for her to continue taking this one day at a time.

To top the morning off, she spoke with both of her boys, delighted to hear their voices and how well they were doing with their summer classes. She'd worried they were taking on too much by going to school year-round, without a summer break, but both had always been driven to push themselves, whether it was with academics or sports. She gave credit to that admirable trait to their father. They'd grown up with Peter's determination to rise to the top of the financial ladder taking precedence over everything else, including the three of them. Thinking back, it amazed her they'd turned out so well adjusted. Neither had taken sides in the divorce, which didn't bother her. The last thing she'd wanted was a rift between them and Peter or her.

As Mia dressed for church, it dawned on her this was the first time she was going into town without dreading the possibility of running into Peter and Tami. Even though they had attended the same church together while married, her ex had yet to make a return to Sunday services. And even if he did, Nolan's undivided attention these past few weeks succeeded in instilling a growing confidence inside her she thought she'd never regain. It wasn't back one hundred percent, but enough she didn't cringe away from the risk of seeing them together again.

Now, she thought as she trotted downstairs and out to her truck, if Barry showed up for work this afternoon and she heard positive news about her delayed shipment, she would start the new week on a high note. What more could she ask for?

Slipping into church, she spotted Dee and Bob and took a seat next to them, idly wondering if Nolan ever attended a service. Given everything they'd done, it made her fidget over how little she knew about the man she was sleeping with. He'd mentioned having dinner with his widowed mother once a week, and that it was just the two of them now. As the parent of the town's reformed bad boy and now top law enforcer, Mrs. MacGregor was well-known around Whitetail, as her husband had been before he passed away. As many stories of Nolan's misspent, wild youth that had filtered down through the years, she'd never heard of one negative episode between him and his parents. There was a lot to admire about him she was just now admitting.

"What are you thinking about? It's not the sermon that's putting that look on your face," Dee whispered, her voice laced with humor.

"Hush."

"Tell me later?"

Mia flicked her an amused glance. "Maybe."

When the service ended, Dee spoke a few quiet words to Bob, who nodded before following the congregation out the front doors as Mia rose and started toward the back to set up the coffee and donuts. "I told you I would cover for you," she reminded Dee who accompanied her into the gathering room used for small socials.

"I know, and I appreciate it, but I'm not busy and we haven't talked in a while. Everybody's wagging their tongues about you and our hot police chief, you know."

That was the most concerning part of her new relationship, despite how much she enjoyed Nolan's attentions. Shaking her head, Mia filled the three coffee pots, uttering, "I hate being the subject of small-town gossip. It was horrible during our split and divorce."

"I know, hon." Dee pitched in and started opening the boxes of donated confectionaries, the sweet aroma of sugar glaze and chocolate permeating the air. "But you've got to admit this kind of gossip is much more fun."

"Maybe for you, but I'm the one people were whispering about, pitying and even blaming for Peter's unfaithfulness. And now, what's left of my reputation is getting tarnished by these rumors." And Mia honestly didn't know how she felt about that regardless of the enlightening experiences Nolan was giving her.

"I figured Peter's affair had already knocked you off that pedestal you put yourself on," Dee returned bluntly before biting into a cream-filled treat with a moan.

It had, so why was she still bemoaning her fall? *More like lamenting my stupidity rather than toppling from the perch of virtue I struggled so hard to climb to after we married in such haste.* That thought shook her. During the early years of her marriage, it had been important for people to see her as a devoted, committed wife and mother, not the teen forced to marry in haste. The birth of the boys ensured she never regretted her relationship with Peter, but she still cared what others thought of her.

"I don't like anyone to think bad of me," she defended herself.

Dee turned and hugged her, almost smearing the last bite of donut on Mia's blouse. "*No one* could ever think bad of you. And if they do, they'll answer to me. I gotta run. Bob's waiting for me. Call me later, since it *would* be unseemly to give me all the salacious details in church."

Mia laughed, shaking her head. "Get out of here."

Within seconds of Dee leaving, several people entered, and the next thirty minutes flew by as Mia enjoyed socializing again. For over a year, she'd kept to herself, too worried about appearances or whether anyone would look down upon her because of Peter's actions. Between that insecurity and the mortification of learning about his deceit, she'd stuck with her closest friends and become a homebody when not working. Her business put her in contact with others, but it was easier to maintain her composure when working, and in truth, no one had treated her differently after the divorce; it had been her own low self-esteem responsible for keeping herself aloof from others.

She'd been basking in the friendly greetings and banter and calling herself an idiot for staying to herself for so long when Tami walked in with another young woman instead of with Peter. Squaring her shoulders, Mia vowed to ignore her, remain polite and unaffected by her presence. Standing behind the long table where two boxes of donuts still waited to be delved into, she forced a smile as the two girls strolled up, surprised Tami would approach her without Peter.

"Good morning. Help yourselves to some donuts. Can I pour you coffee or juice?" she inquired in as polite a tone as she could muster. The crowd was dwindling rapidly and the few people still loitering in small groups didn't appear interested in seeing the ex-wife and new fiancée talking, which helped ease her tension until Tami answered in a snide undertone.

"I'll have a cup of coffee, plain. If I indulged in such calorie-laden food, I wouldn't be able to get into my clothes." With an insolent look, she smirked at her friend. "Is it any wonder Peter looked elsewhere for his... needs?"

Shock held Mia's tongue for several seconds as a blush crept over her face. She couldn't believe the insolent audacity of the chit, and how easily Tami maintained her friendly mien while delivering such a rude comment to Mia's face. Determined to be the better person here, she bit back the retort on the tip of her tongue and conjured a smile as she poured the coffee.

"Here you go. Can I get you anything else?"

Tami laughed. "No, hon. I already have everything I ever

wanted from you. And I know how to keep him. You must come by and see what I've done to the house. You won't recognize it."

Several heads turned at the sound of Tami's raised voice and Mia wished the floor would open and swallow her as a few faces reflected pity, with some frowns aimed at Tami and her smirking friend. Hurt and anger fought to be unleashed on the other woman, but before she could think of anything to say to her, the two of them sauntered out looking smug, as if her stunned silence was exactly what they'd expected of her.

How Mia managed to maintain her composure as she cleaned up, she didn't know. Keeping her face averted from the few people still mingling, she tossed the empty donut boxes and placed the remaining ones in the refrigerator. It didn't take but a minute to unplug and rinse out the coffee pots and by the time she made one final sweep of the room for trash, no one else remained. No one mentioned the incident and several smiled and tossed out a *goodbye* or *see you next week* as they left, but her temper still simmered under the layer of pain Tami's calloused words caused.

Mia didn't love Peter anymore, hadn't for a long time, so it wasn't the mention of Tami having him now that hurt, but the house that held all the memories of where she'd raised her boys that cut through her like a lance piercing her heart. She didn't know whether she ached more from that pain or from suppressing the urge to lower herself to Tami's level and lash back at her. Tears of anger and frustration blinded her way as she got into her truck and headed back to the nursery.

She stayed inside the shop most of the afternoon, leaving the guys to handle the customers. Her mood vacillated between bristling resentment over Tami's public dressing down and despair over everything she'd lost. Telling herself losing material objects, such as the house, couldn't rob her of her memories did little to soothe Mia in her agitated state. At least Barry had shown up today, and all three offered to come in tomorrow if the delayed shipment arrived. The eager way they'd jumped in to help her out reminded her how lucky she was, but she still wasn't in the mood to play nice when Nolan showed up with attitude written in the tight set of his five-o'clock shadowed jaw and anger snapping in his cobalt eyes just as she was closing.

THE SATED, contented woman Nolan left that morning was nowhere around when he walked into the shop, and Mia's attitude fit right in with his annoyance with her. After spending the past few weeks showing her she had no reason to cower from that prick of an ex and his immature side-piece, it pissed him off when he got wind of the nasty scene between Mia and Tami at her church. He waited for his deputy to tell him how Mia laid into the younger woman, but learned that wasn't the case, and damn it, he wanted to know why.

Slamming the door behind him, he leaned against it, glad to see the taillights of the hired hands' car leaving. Folding his arms, he returned Mia's glare as he demanded, "Why the fuck didn't you tell the bitch off?"

"What?" Enlightenment dawned, and her face paled before turning bright red. "Gee, Chief, I never knew you were so fond of gossip."

"Cut the attitude, Mia." Pushing away from the door, he stalked across the room and braced his hands on the counter separating them. "Haven't I showed you that girl has nothing on you? What the hell is it going to take to get you to open your eyes and see you're worth ten times what she is?"

Slamming the till drawer shut, her green eyes turned frigid as she snapped, "It's easy for you to berate me, but you've never been humiliated the way I have, never lost the house you raised your children in or had people you've known your whole life look at you with pity because you were too stupid to see what was right in front of your face!"

Mia clamped her mouth shut, and he could tell by her appalled look she couldn't believe she'd revealed those innermost feelings of inadequacy to him. Coming around the counter, he decided it was time to set her straight on a few things. Snatching her hand, he asked, "Where's your office?"

"Why?"

Her suspicious tone tugged at his lips even though he was irritated as hell with her. "Because I don't think you want me to bend you over out here even though everyone has gone for the day." She yanked on her hand, but her pulse leapt under his fingers.

"What's gotten into you? You can't mean to… just because…." She stuttered down the short hall until he turned her and pressed her shoulders down on the desk in her office.

Nolan noticed she didn't fight him *too* much but did swivel her crimson face around to glare at him. "What's gotten into me is you, apparently. Yes, I can mean to punish you for your idiocy in thinking you were the stupid one in handling your marriage." Yanking down her shorts and panties, he delivered a hard swat on her right buttock. "You're ten times better than that twit your dick of an ex has taken up with." He smacked her left cheek. "Repeat after me. I was not at fault." *Slap! Slap! Slap!*

Mia shifted her hips and turned her face away but muttered, "I was not at fault."

He belabored the tender area of her sit-spots with his next demand. "Repeat I was an idiot for letting her get to me."

With a whimper, she lowered her head, shifted her feet and whispered, "I was an idiot for letting her get to me."

Grabbing her braid, Nolan yanked her head up and covered her bouncing globes with a rapid volley of blistering swats, alternating between berating her and praising her with each one. "You *are* stupid if you continue to let that girl goad you." Two blows on her right cheek. "I love fucking you, Mia. You're a submissive delight any man would sell his right nut to have under his control." A blistering slap to her upper left thigh. "Quit behaving as if they matter, because, God damn it, they don't."

Neither of them heard the bell clang over the door or the footsteps coming down the hall.

"What is going on here?" Peter's shocked voice surprised both of them, but Nolan turned to him with a sneer as he released Mia's hair and pressed one hand between her shoulders to keep her in place and switched from belaboring her ass to caressing the hot, reddened globes.

"Stay still," he instructed, his eyes staying on Peter where the other man stood gaping at her naked, abused ass. "None of your business, is it, sweetheart?"

MIA COULDN'T BELIEVE she wasn't jumping up in mortification to cover herself in front of Peter. But Master Nolan possessed a way of driving home his point, as her throbbing, abused backside could attest to. As soon as he'd donned his Dom persona, her heart had tripped with excitement, her palms dampening in expectation as her pussy wept. Between those telltale responses and his words, she'd turned to putty under his hard hand while realizing everything he was drilling into her was right. It was time she quit taking the blame for what her prick of an ex was responsible for.

Nolan caressed her heated cheeks, his softer touch soothing her raw nerves while fortifying her courage to face Peter where he stood rooted in the doorway. "That's right, this—me—is none of your concern, so go away." Just to taunt him, she wiggled her butt and grinned. "I'm busy."

"This... Mia, that's just... wrong. I demand you release her, MacGregor. What would people think—"

"You've got to be kidding!" Mia burst out on an incredulous laugh. "God, I never realized what a hypocrite you are."

"As you can see," Nolan put in as he continued to fondle her aching backside. "Mia is a willing participant here. In fact, I was just going to finish up this lesson with my belt."

She heard the sound of him pulling the thick leather off his waist and then the caress of warmed leather ghosted a trail over her quivering buttocks. "Oh, God," she moaned, a shiver of longing rippling down her spine. "Get out, Peter." Turning her face away from his angry scowl and splotchy red face, she relished listening to his heavy stomping down the hall followed by the slamming of the door.

"I'm proud of you Mia."

Nolan's praise wrapped around her like a warm hug as he trailed the belt up between her legs. "Does that mean you're *not* going to use that on me?"

"No."

The belt slashed across her buttocks, leaving a swath of fiery pain that sent her senses reeling. With a cry that echoed around the room, she accepted each of the five strokes biting into her flesh. While embracing the seeping pleasure spiraling through her lower body, Mia struggled to maintain her composure over the way he'd handled Peter's intrusion, sticking up for her while keeping her in place with the hand between her shoulders and the one caressing her butt. But giving her the chance to do the same for herself topped off everything else. By the time she heard the belt drop to the floor and his zipper lower, the tears pricking her eyes weren't solely from the pulsating pain encompassing her backside.

Her pussy, already filled with liquid heat, welcomed the invasion of his sheathed cock, her hips dancing in tune with his womb-bumping plunges. A tight coil gripped her stomach as sensation built with each plummeting thrust, his harsh breathing mingling with her desperate gasps.

Nolan slowed long enough to work two fingers into her rectum. "I've been fantasizing about fucking your tight ass, maybe in my office, with my staff on the other side of the door." She gushed over his cock at the erotic suggestion and his low laugh mortified her further. "I've said it before, but it bears repeating. You continue to surprise me, sweetheart. I love that. The plug has been helping, you're much looser."

Mia hadn't quibbled over his insistence she insert the anal toy for an hour each day and now was glad she'd obeyed. He pulled out of her tight orifice and she couldn't wait another second to let go. "Master, *please*," she pleaded in a whispery voice she knew and didn't care revealed the height of her need.

"Took you long enough," Nolan grunted behind her, his hands grabbing her hips and holding them still for the forceful finish of his possession.

Her mind blurring with the overflow of sensation, Mia squeezed his thick girth as she exploded in climax, felt the jerks of his hot come jetting inside her and basked in the knowledge she could bring him the same pleasure as he did her.

She was still trying to catch her breath when he helped her up and pulled up her shorts. "How long will it take you to get ready?"

"For what?" she asked with lazy interest as she leaned against him for support.

"It's prime rib night at the diner, and I'm starving."

And just like that, the strict Dom slid away, replaced by a regular guy ruled by his stomach. Was it any wonder she liked him?

"I can be ready in fifteen minutes. That sounds good."

Chapter 10

"And I'm still telling you you're wrong, Chuck." Nolan gripped the phone tighter and swiveled his chair toward the window behind his desk. Preparations were hammering away for the citywide picnic this weekend, but this call put an end to his enthusiasm for attending with Mia.

His former boss's exaggerated sigh came through the phone loud and clear. "I'll let you know. We have people tracking several trucks headed for three different nurseries in New Mexico, and The Greenleaf Nursery is on the list. Mia Reynolds and her place stay on our radar," Chuck insisted.

"If you're targeting two other nurseries in different cities that means they have a ring going that has to involve inside sources at each stop." The sick churning in Nolan's gut was a sign his suspicions about who at Mia's nursery might be the inside person there were right on target. He usually prided himself on his accurate intuitions. Not this time. "Look, I know her. It wouldn't surprise me if she's being used, but I guarantee she knows nothing about it."

"I believe you, but I still have to follow the leads, and so do you. Keep looking."

"Fine. But I didn't see anything untoward at her nursery and I'm sticking by my assertion Mia is not involved in any way."

Nolan hung up and strode out of his office with frustration eating away at his insides. This fucking investigation had put forwarding his relationship with Mia on hold almost since it started and now placed it in jeopardy. And that was unacceptable. He'd pursued her with the sole purpose of exploring the hint of submissiveness and interest he'd glimpsed that one time, a look he hadn't been able to forget no matter how many years passed or how much distance separated them. Scratching that itch was all he'd intended at first, but somewhere along the way, the cock-stirring prickly side of Mia had merged with her surfacing submissiveness and heightened responses to meld into a woman he continued to crave more of. Could there be a more perfect combination when he added in her admirable determination to make a successful go of her business despite her evident low self-esteem that constantly kept her questioning her self-worth?

They'd been seen together in public and it pissed him off when she would shy away from anyone who'd been friends with both her and Peter. The woman who walked around blaming herself for her husband's infidelity was so completely at odds with the attitude-driven woman who'd kept him at arm's length for months, was it any wonder his dominant side insisted he take her in hand? She'd blossomed into a sensuous woman under his tutoring and had taken the first step toward putting that prick in his place the other day in her office. But it wasn't enough, not by a long shot.

"Hank, Morgan. There's a three-car accident blocking traffic out on the highway at Miller Road. No injuries but a damned bottleneck. Go see what you can do," he instructed his two most seasoned deputies.

"You got it, Chief." Morgan stood and grabbed his hat without questions. Hank nodded and followed him out.

"Everything okay, Chief?" Carrie, the dispatcher, looked up at him with concern clouding her face.

"Yeah, for now, Carrie. Thanks." He returned to his office praying it stayed that way.

"WHAT NOW?" Clifton looked up from the numbers swimming before him and glared at Sanchez's rude intrusion into his office. "Knocking would be nice."

"Fuck being nice and fuck you if you think I'm taking the rap for you," his pain-in-the-ass hired hand snapped.

"Can you be a little clearer?"

"I can be clear as glass." Stomping across the room, he leaned his hands on the desk and snarled down at him. "Word is the Feds are on our ass. How's that for clear?"

Swearing a blue streak, Clifton forced himself to rein in his temper. Imbeciles. He was surrounded by them. He may have waited too long to sever ties with his current associates. "Stand back, Sanchez. I haven't gotten this far by being stupid. There's nothing that can lead them to us, as I've repeatedly told you."

Straightening, Raul crossed his arms and said, "The Reynolds bitch can put me with one of her guys."

Clifton shrugged. "So?"

"So, it's not you putting your ass on the line meeting up with all these connections."

Some placating would be necessary if he wanted to keep Sanchez in line for the next few weeks while he figured out what to do next. He despised the necessity, but he would continue to do whatever was required to save his land. "You have my word we'll pull out of this if anything points in your direction. In the meantime, I'll double your bonus on the next shipment, which should be ready in the next few days. I told you I'd always have your back."

"See that you do, *boss*."

BY THE TIME Saturday morning rolled around and Mia was slipping back into her apartment after spending another night being tormented in Nolan's decadent bondage room and then waking sore and sated in his bed, she was more than ready to socialize at the annual town picnic. She'd missed last year's Fourth of July celebration for the first time. She and Peter had just split, and she'd chosen to stay home in shame rather than hear a lot of platitudes and contend with a slew of pitying looks. Thanks to her friends' constant prodding and Nolan's influence, she was done with putting her life on hold.

The week had started on a sour note when she'd gotten word her shipment would be delayed until at least next week. Since a good amount of her foliage came from horticultural farms in Mexico, it hadn't been the first time she'd suffered the frustration of such a wait, something she'd learned could happen when she'd researched this career choice. At least she'd ended the week on a high note after Nolan talked her into taking yesterday off to drive up to Santa Fe and visit the boys. Playing hooky from work the day before they closed for the town's festivities had felt good. What felt even better was spending the entire day with both him and her sons after he'd insisted on accompanying her.

Watching Nolan's easy, comfortable interaction with her boys, as if he'd known them for years, edged up her like of the man yet another notch. She still shied away from thinking about how many notches remained before like tumbled into something much stronger.

With only a few hours until Nolan picked her up, Mia sat down to catch up on bills before putting together her popular spaghetti pie casserole to bake while she showered. By the time she'd braided her hair and dressed in a summer, calf-length skirt of swirling pleated blues and plain white tank top, she heard him coming up the stairs and rushed to greet him. Flinging open the door, her pulse jumped as if she hadn't seen him in days instead of hours and her body warmed just from the look in his vivid blue gaze when he tipped his hat back.

"Why do you have your hair pulled back?" he asked with a frown as she held the door open.

Mia rolled her eyes behind his back. "I've told you. It's too hot to wear it down all day, especially outside."

Without looking back at her, he ordered, "Stop rolling your eyes and pull up your top." Fishing a small vial out of his pocket, he pivoted to face her again.

She eyed the tube with wariness as she shut the door. "We're going to a city picnic. You do remember how many people attend every year, don't you?"

Not trusting the gleam in his eyes, she backed up as he walked slowly toward her until her calves bumped against the sofa. "I assume it draws as big a crowd as I recall. What's your point?" he drawled, using his other hand to tug her top free of the skirt.

Mia narrowed her eyes at him when he released the front catch on her bra and her breasts sprang free, her nipples puckering from the sudden waft of cooler air and the banked heat in his eyes. "You're making me uncomfortable by being deliberately obtuse." She held her breath as he popped the cap and the scent of cinnamon permeated the space between them.

"I like you uncomfortable. It makes your capitulation all that much sweeter. Relax." Nolan smiled as he brushed her right nipple with a cream-coated finger. "Cinnamon oil is popular for a slow, but intense warm-up. My previous subs loved it." His damn grin widened when she narrowed her eyes at his mention of other women.

Mia suffered through a thorough coating of each tender nub, and the warm tingling sensation the gel induced. Her relief when he fastened her bra and tugged down her tank top was short-lived. Setting the oil aside, he spun her around by the shoulders and bent her over the couch.

"I neglected to mention it's labeled a clit sensitizer. You'll like this as much, if not more, than what you're feeling now."

She didn't comment on Nolan's smug tone; she'd learned he was always right in these matters. After draping her skirt over her back and lowering her panties, he executed a slow, thorough search to root out her clit, forcing her shuddering breath when he covered the aching bud with the cinnamon oil gel.

A pleasant but distracting warmth invaded her pussy and set her clit to throbbing in tune with her softly pulsating nipples as he slid his finger between her buttocks to wipe the remaining oil on her anus. "You can't mean for me to parade around in a crowd all afternoon in this state?" she fretted when he righted her clothes and she turned to confront him with a flaming face.

"You'll be fine. I can't wait to taste whatever smells so good."

"Crap! I forgot about the casserole." Mia dashed into the kitchen and pulled the bubbling dish from the oven. Ignoring both Nolan and her traitorous body, she covered the pan and placed it in an insulated carrier before facing him again. Taking a deep breath, praying she was right, she stated, "I'm ready."

NOLAN NODDED, needing this relaxed, fun time with Mia in the worst way. His conscience had pricked him with guilt each time he'd stopped at her nursery on the pretext of visiting her instead of looking for evidence drugs were being snuck by her among her inventory. You could smack him in the face with irrefutable proof of her involvement, and he still wouldn't believe it. Her expressions and actions read like an open book regarding every aspect of her life. What they'd shared these past few weeks convinced him there was no way she could have hidden such a thing from him.

Parking in his reserved slot at the police station, Nolan snatched Mia's hand before strolling toward the festivity-packed park behind the building. "Bob signed me up to play on his softball team," he stated, veering toward the ball field. "I warned him I haven't played in ages, but he insisted."

"I used to play on a women's league, years ago." The wistful note in her voice revealed how much she missed that activity.

"Why did you quit?"

Her green gaze slid to a small group standing by the bandstand. He recognized both Peter and the young woman her ex was dumb enough to dump Mia for. "Peter preferred me to spend my spare time working on the town's welcoming guild and charity fundraisers." She shrugged as they approached the bleachers. "Between that and the twins, I didn't have time for anything else."

"Well, you're no longer with the prick and I think you should do what pleases you."

She flicked him a sly look. "Like insisting we go someplace private and you do something about ending my torment?"

Nolan leaned in to her, uncaring about the people watching as he fisted his hand around her braid and tugged her head back to assault her smiling mouth. Mia sank against him, a positive sign she was much more relaxed and accepting of him and his dominance in front of others. Was it any wonder he was crazy about her after such a short time?

He kept the kiss short but thorough and by the time he released her, her face was flushed, her eyes dilated. Bending to her ear, he whispered, "Is that look from my mouth or the effects of the cinnamon oil?"

Her low laugh vibrated against his chest. "Both, you moron." Shoving against his chest, she admonished, "Go play ball."

He did but found it difficult to concentrate with Mia sitting next to Dee on the bleachers, hearing her root him on. Maybe it had been a mistake to play with her before leaving. At this point, he wasn't sure his actions weren't tormenting him more than her. How they managed to win the game, he didn't know, but by the end of the ninth inning, he stirred in hunger for more than a plateful of the food laid out on the long tables by the picnic area.

"DAMN, HE'S HOT," Dee sighed, her eyes not on her husband but the chief of police. *Mia's* chief of police, at least for now.

She sighed and pushed to her feet, her tingling, toasty girl parts turning hotter as she watched Nolan saunter toward her with a wicked grin curling his lips and a gleam in his cobalt eyes she knew not to trust. Not that her slutty libido cared. "Yeah, he is." For about the thousandth time, she wondered what he was doing with her, and she with him.

Dee's smile turned into a frown. "Anything wrong?"

Mia shook her head. "No, just reminding myself nothing good ever lasts."

"That's not true," Dee argued. "Look at me and Bob."

"You guys are the exception to the rule. It doesn't matter though since I'm not in the market for anything permanent. This suits me just fine for the time being."

Nolan slung his arm around her shoulders when he and Bob joined them, his warm, perspiring body pressed against her side driving the simmering need inside her higher. "What suits you just fine?"

"Being seen with someone from the winning team, of course," she quipped. His dubious look said he didn't believe her, but thankfully he let it go.

"Excuse us for a few minutes, would you?" he addressed Dee and Bob. "I need to do my civic duty and make the rounds. If you can wait, we'll join you in the buffet line in about thirty minutes."

"Sounds good." Bob nodded.

Much to Mia's chagrin, Nolan kept her close as they strolled around, stopping to visit with people enjoying the games, music and food. Her body flooded with awareness of his muscled strength and possessive touches as well as the looks ranging between surprised and envious women were sending her way. When she shifted her gaze to a group of women from the welcome guild and Darla Atkins, her and Peter's next-door neighbor, gave her a thumbs up with a wide grin of approval, Mia basked in the unexpected sign of encouragement.

"Where are we going?" she asked when she noticed Nolan had maneuvered her back around to the police station fifteen minutes later.

"To get out of this heat for a few minutes." Catching on to the urgency reflected in his tone, she quickened her steps to match his, her pulse rate jumping twenty points as they entered the deserted building.

"Don't you need someone to man the phones?" she panted as he all but hauled her behind him down the hall to his office.

"Emergency calls are being routed to the two deputies on call."

Shutting the door behind him, Nolan left the room in shadows cast by the semi-closed window blinds. Music, shrieks of laughter and kids squealing in fun seeped through the walls. Knowing friends were just a few feet outside this room titillated Mia on a whole new level. The sudden urge to give back to *Master* Nolan in appreciation of all he'd done for her, and to her, sent her to her knees before him. His startled look was her last glimpse of his face before she released his cock into her hands and bent her head.

"This time you have to take what I dish out." She closed her mouth around his cockhead and swirled her tongue over the smooth, velvet soft crown. The low, guttural moan that escaped his mouth as he gripped her braid, gave her a boost in the confidence she still lacked. The tight clasp of his other hand on her shoulder aided in steadying her as she released him to explore his rigid shaft with both hands.

"I like touching you." Mia heard the wonder of that in her voice but couldn't help spilling the honest revelation. Peter's sex had never fascinated her as much as Nolan's.

"I'm glad, but I'll still punish you for trying to take the lead here," he warned in a guttural tone that went straight to her empty, needy core.

Mia's lips curved as she flicked her eyes up to his taut face. "You would probably do that regardless."

Nolan yanked on her braid and thrust up toward her mouth. "Brat. Get back to what you were doing. We don't have much time and I intend to take your ass this afternoon."

She swallowed past her dry throat as a hunger coursed through her body from that bold statement, one she knew only he could sate. Hard and hot, his cock seared her palm, his cobalt gaze burning through her defenses. Mia could feel his blood pumping through the thick veins as she explored his thickness, her palm coated with his slippery seepage. His urgency matched the fire pulsing against her clit as she followed with her mouth and took him in deep. He didn't give her much time to savor his taste on her tongue, scrape her teeth along the throbbing, blood-pumping veins, or enjoy the way his girth stretched her lips; only a few slurping, head-bobbing moments to torment him before yanking her head back, drawing her to her feet and propelling her over to the desk.

"I liked the way you looked lying over your desk, your ass exposed and mine to do with as I please." He urged her down and she took up the same position, reaching across the desk to grip the other side as he flipped up her skirt and dropped her panties. Her buttocks tightened when he ran his hand over them in a fondling caress. "Trying to keep me out, sweetheart? I would think you'd learned by now how futile that is."

"You'd think," Mia mumbled under her breath, keeping her face buried between her stretched arms. Her nipples, pussy and anus already palpitated with warmth from the cinnamon oil, but this position heightened her awareness of her lower body, and what he meant to do with it. A jumbled mix of nerves and excitement skittered under her skin, causing butterflies to flutter in her abdomen as she held her breath and waited.

The smack on bare flesh resonated in the room and she welcomed the distracting sting and now familiar burn, blew out her breath with the next swat and sucked it back in with the blistering force of the third. Now her buttocks throbbed with heat along with her other tidbits. She gasped as he drove her onto her toes, working three fingers into her sopping sheath, taking his time pumping inside her with teasing glides over her aching clit. When he pulled out and trailed up her crack to spear into her tight anus with cream-coated fingers, reality faded, and the invasion of a raw sexual hunger took command of her senses.

"You'll be tight, but you can take me now." Nolan paused to withdraw slowly from her ass and apply a liberal dose of cool lube, his ministrations loosening her rectum muscles even more. "Deep breath, Mia," he warned as she heard him sheath his cock and then felt the slick head of his penis pushing against her rear entrance.

Squeezing her eyes shut, she inhaled and tried not to tense, wanting this, but fearing the unknown. His deep voice aided in relaxing her as he worked his way past her tight resistance.

"Slow and easy. You're safe with me, sweetheart. Always." She burned from the gentle stretch, but every raw nerve came alive with scintillating pleasure with each deep press. "There, halfway is all I'll go. Breathe," he coaxed. "I don't want you passing out unless it's from climaxing."

Mia would've laughed but Nolan began jabbing in and out of

her butt with short thrusts, the hand not clamped on her hip finding its way to her pussy, his fingers to her clit. She trembled from the dichotomy of riotous sensations he whipped up with this taboo act. Flames engulfed her entire crotch, front to back as he continued to plunder both orifices until she exploded into mindless ecstasy. She felt the jerk of his own release, but he never let up from milking her clit and plundering her rectum until they both lay spent and gasping.

NOLAN RESTED on top of Mia, struggling to catch his breath and clear his head. His thighs pressed against her warm buttocks and his still spewing cock lay snuggled inside the tight confines of her hot ass. Fuck, but that felt good. Her brave and generous trust in him to take care of her during that new and likely frightening experience left him humbled. She hadn't questioned or balked as he'd half expected even though he'd been preparing her for anal sex almost from their first night together. He doubted she realized the significance of that, but he did. Because he did, the urgency to end his part in the drug investigation just became even more paramount.

Whether or not she was ready to admit it aloud, this was not just an affair. It was more than he'd planned on, definitely more than she'd bargained for, but he wouldn't let that stop him from forging ahead.

"That's my girl," Nolan praised her when they strolled over to the food tables and she kept her head high and a smile on her face despite a few questioning glances. "Let them wonder where we've been. I bet most are speculating with envy."

Mia shook her head at him. "You've lived in D.C. too long. Small town gossip can harm my business."

"Doubtful, yet you believe that and are still with me. Think about that, sweetheart. There's Bob and Dee." Nolan could tell by the look on her face his comment had struck a chord. She needed to give serious thought to them as a couple because he intended to forge ahead in cementing their relationship.

NOLAN WAS RIGHT, Mia mused as she returned Dee's knowing smirk when they met up in the food court. Somewhere along the way, she had ceased worrying about her business reputation, choosing instead to get as much out of the time he allotted her as possible.

"I want *every* detail," Dee demanded in her ear as Mia picked up a paper plate and plastic utensils.

"Later, you nut," she whispered back, praying no one else had heard. Mia glanced down the table and spotted Trish filling her plate along with a good-looking man she didn't recognize. Her young assistant winked just as Nolan looked her way.

The grin splitting his sun-bronzed face was easy to see even though he'd donned his hat again when they'd left the precinct. "I do believe Trish approves," he stated aloud.

Mia kicked his shin and gave him a mock glare even though a small grin hovered on her lips. "She just likes teasing me. Get moving, I'm hungry."

For the first time since her split from Peter, Mia enjoyed an afternoon with the people she'd known most of her life. She even managed not to stumble or back away whenever Peter and Tami walked by or were conversing with someone she'd just enjoyed talking to. It had been easy to avoid them, but when seventy-something Mrs. Zimmerman, the high school's retired math teacher, leaned on her cane and said, "You go, girl," with a sly glance toward Nolan, it was the final boost to Mia's confidence that prepared her to meet Peter's criticism head on when it came.

A group of men hailed Nolan to join a rope pulling contest and Mia had just waved him off and started toward the spectators when Peter stepped into her path, waylaying her without Tami by his side. Grabbing her arm, he surprised her when he pulled her aside and hissed, "You're making a spectacle of yourself!"

His hypocritical chastisement burst the final dam on holding her emotions in check, and she erupted into laughing until tears rolled down her face. "May...be Tami has... been good for you. You... you never used to... have a sense of... humor!"

"Mia, damn it, this is not funny." He cast a look around, as always, maintaining propriety in public as his main concern.

"Yes, it is." Mia sobered, eyed her ex with wonder over what she ever saw in him, and shook her head. "Fuck off, Peter. What I do is no longer your business. Tami is welcome to you."

She walked away from his astonished look without glancing back, feeling lighter than she had in ages. When she reached Dee, who stood watching with several others as five men lined up at each end of a long thick rope began pulling each other over a man-made mud pit, her heart stuttered when Nolan glanced up and nodded. The look on his face told her he'd been watching her speak with Peter and approved of how she'd handled herself without even knowing what she'd said.

Damn, she really, really liked that man.

Chapter 11

The enjoyable weekend came to a crashing halt the next day. Five minutes before opening, Mia's phone pealed, displaying Drew's number. Since none of them were here, ready to work, she didn't bother to disguise her irritation or impatience when she answered.

"You better have a damn good excuse."

"I do. It's Barry. He's… he's in the hospital. They think it's an overdose." Drew's young voice broke, turning soft and scared. "*Shit, shit, shit.*"

Dumbfounded, Mia lowered herself to the chair behind the counter in the shop, rubbing her brow as quick tears pricked her eyes. Despite her complaints about Barry, her heart ached hearing about his condition. How had she missed his drug use? The question nagged at her as she got the details from Drew, excused both him and Donny from work and jotted down the hospital in Albuquerque where she planned to visit him this evening.

Trish came in as she hung up, took one look at her face and asked, "What's up?"

After Mia relayed what she knew, Trish also appeared

surprised to hear Barry was using. "I never saw a sign. If he'd ever showed up here high, I know one of us would have noticed."

"That's what I think, too." Mia rose, sadness and a sense of urgency prodding her to call her sons. She needed to hear their voices and ensure they were okay. "Go ahead and open. If you can manage in here alone today, I'll take care of outside. I'd planned to make up for closing yesterday by tending to Birmingham's landscaping job, but that'll have to wait."

"He'll understand. I've always thought him a nice guy."

"Thank goodness. Today is not the day to have to deal with a contrary customer."

Clifton assured her his job could wait and the concern in his voice over Barry's condition helped ease Mia's conscience about putting the remainder of his lucrative contract on hold. A few afternoon customers asked about the guy's absence, and since no one mentioned hearing about Barry's overdose, she didn't bring it up. She'd forgotten how grueling running the nursery practically by herself could be and was feeling the effects by closing time. The afternoon had passed so fast due to the steady business, she didn't catch Nolan's text, 'Tied up with work until late' until she waved Trish off a little after 5:00. She prayed whatever was keeping him busy on a Sunday had nothing to do with the drug case plaguing their county, and that Barry's circumstances weren't a result of those tainted drugs.

The disappointment Nolan's cryptic message elicited added to her growing belief their relationship was moving in a new direction. That thought didn't worry her as much as before; in fact, the idea of settling into another commitment warmed her where Peter had left her so cold for so long. *Who would've thought?*

The silence in the shop and then yard as she trotted upstairs produced an uneasy curl of dread in her abdomen for no explicable reason, the sudden queasiness erasing the pleasant glow of her musings. Shaking off the weird sense of doom, she took a quick shower, putting off getting something to eat until after she'd checked up on Barry.

Mia didn't care for hospitals; the sterile atmosphere, the smell of anesthetic, lack of natural sunlight and odors of sickness and drugs made her crave to be outdoors. She was the most content when the sun was warming her skin and her hands were buried in the soil or tending to nature's bounty. The shiver of foreboding she experienced earlier returned as she rode the elevator up to the fourth floor, increased as she strode down the hall toward Barry's room, and settled into a hard knot cramping her abdomen when she spotted Nolan conversing with another man.

Since Barry resided in Albuquerque, Nolan's presence could only mean her young employee had gotten hold of the tainted drugs he was investigating and trying to stop. Her chest constricted as she recalled the young man who'd died from his ingestion of the same product. The look in Nolan's eyes when he saw her confirmed her fears.

"The drugs were bad?" she asked as soon as she reached them.

He nodded. "Yes, we already have the lab report. I'm sorry, Mia. He's critical, in a coma, but at least he's still alive." Turning to the shorter, older man next to him, he introduced her. "Chuck Campbell, DEA. This is Mia Reynolds." The pointed look Nolan turned on the other man as Chuck held out his hand did nothing to dispel the apprehension still twisting inside her.

"Nice to meet you," Mia lied, shaking his hand. She wanted nothing to do with the Feds because that would bring their work much too close to her beloved hometown than she cared for.

"Ms. Reynolds. Chief MacGregor tells me Barry is your employee."

"Yes, but before you ask, no, I've never known him to show up for work under the influence of any illegal substance." She couldn't stifle the urge to defend Barry. From the moment she'd hired all three college students, she'd tried not to think of them as someone's sons, or as she did her own boys, and that any bad behavior when they weren't at work was not her problem or a reflection on her. But those efforts had refused to stick. "Barry, and his two friends who also work for me, are twenty-one and like to go clubbing on the weekends. Do you think someone slipped something into his drink?"

Both hesitated before Nolan answered. "We're not ruling anything out yet." He grasped her elbow, telling Chuck, "Excuse us a minute."

Chuck nodded. "I have to get going. I'll be in touch. Mia, it was nice to meet you."

Mia waited until the agent reached the elevator before rounding on Nolan in suspicion. "What aren't you telling me?"

"Nothing. You know I can't comment on an ongoing investigation. Barry's family is in with him and have requested time to themselves. Have you eaten?"

Frustration shimmered off him in waves but Mia put it down to the case. Wishing she could ease his burden somehow, she shoved aside her misgivings and that new, enlightening tidbit to ponder over later. "No. I intended to grab something on the way back."

"I'm in the mood for something with a bite to it. How about Taqueria's?"

"Never been but heard of it. I could go for Mexican." *And you.*

NOLAN GENTLY DISENGAGED from Mia's soft, clinging body, snatched his phone off the nightstand and put it to his ear as he grabbed his jeans and slipped out of her room. "MacGregor," he answered as he went into the bathroom and shut the door behind him. "Is he coherent?" he questioned the agent assigned at the hospital. "Give me an hour. I'll contact Agent Campbell. Fine. Tell him I'm on my way."

Tossing the phone on the counter, he washed up and dressed as fast as possible, the cold knot of apprehension that had been cramping his gut ever since he got the call about Barry twisting into an icy snarl. As he'd suspected, the kid was involved with drug runners up to his overdosed neck. While he was thankful over hearing Barry had awakened, and the doctors were now optimistic about his chances, he bemoaned how this would reflect on Mia. There was still no doubt in his mind she was innocent, but if she and her nursery were being used it would devastate her. Not to mention the way he'd kept the possibility from her.

Nolan sent Chuck a quick text when he didn't answer his call, reminding him to hold off on sending the Feds to search Greenleaf Nursery. He needed time to talk to Barry before he broke that news to Mia. Slipping back into the bedroom, he leaned over the bed, slid his hand under the covers and cupped one full breast. Rasping the nipple into a pucker as he nibbled on her lips, he murmured, "Got to run, sweetheart. I'll call you later."

She arched into his hand with a low moan, sighing, "'Kay."

His heart turned over as he pulled back and left her to do his damn job.

MIA WORKED the nursery by herself on Mondays since it was usually the slowest day. Most of the time, she enjoyed the slower business following a busy weekend, but by noon she was ready to climb the walls. The strange bout of anxiety that struck her yesterday returned for no reason, at least that's what she thought until the crunch of multiple vehicles rolling into her yard drew her attention out the shop's front window. Her throat went dry as she watched a dark van with a DEA logo stenciled on the side pull to a stop, followed by two official-looking cars. Several men wearing DEA vests emerged from the vehicles and she recognized Chuck Campbell, the agent Nolan introduced her to yesterday.

The bile churning in her stomach rose in a nauseous rush to her throat as she came around the counter on unsteady legs. Flinging open the door, she met Agent Campbell with a frown, her eyes going to the official looking paper clutched in his hand.

"Ms. Reynolds, I have a warrant to search these premises. We'd appreciate it if you'd stand aside until we finish."

She didn't see the regret in his eye, only saw the men fanning out across her yard and the slow ruin of everything she'd worked so hard for. Tears burned her eyes while disbelief and confusion clouded her mind.

"I don't understand," she whispered, reaching for the warrant with a shaking hand.

"We're searching for evidence your employee, Barry Middleton, has been handing off illegal drugs that were smuggled through with your inventory."

Stunned, Mia sank down onto the step and looked up at him in denial. "That can't be true. I would have known," she insisted, her mind going numb with the jumble of confusing thoughts before one struck her with the force of a double-fisted punch to the abdomen. "Am… am I a suspect?"

Campbell looked away from her, as if he couldn't bear to see her face when he replied, "Let's just say we haven't cleared you."

Sharp talons of fear scraped along her skin, her first thought how this would affect her boys. When Peter left her, she'd thought she'd lost everything. It took a while to realize she hadn't, but now she very well could. Another vehicle came roaring into the lot and screeching to a stop. Mia jumped to her feet when Nolan slammed out of the cruiser, but the furious look he aimed toward Agent Campbell switched to guilt when his gaze swiveled to her, his words cutting her to the bone with the knife-sharp edge of betrayal.

"God damn it, Campbell. I told you to wait!"

Campbell glared at him before joining his team in destroying her dream, but all she could think now was: *he knew*. Those two words reverberated in her head as she grappled with Nolan's deceitful involvement. He reached for her and she stepped away, the thought of him touching her now abhorrent. "Just how long after my nursery came under suspicion did you wait before deciding to seduce me?" Her voice trembled, but she forced her head up and her eyes on him.

His face darkened and the glint that entered his eyes was one that used to produce a shiver of expectation. Not this time. Now, she felt nothing past the numbness of betrayal. Peter's defection had hurt. Nolan's pierced her with such excruciating pain, she knew she would carry the scars forever.

"You know better than that, Mia. Let's go inside…"

She sidled away from his grasp again, slow growing anger worming its way past the shock and grief. "Do I?" She dared a quick peek behind her, cringed at the callous disregard for her inventory and then turned back to face the man responsible. "I believe you have a job to do, Chief MacGregor. If you'll excuse me, I need to phone my lawyer. It looks like you've seen to it I'll need one."

He moved fast enough to snatch her elbow as she turned away and hauled her up against him. She could feel his body vibrating, see the conflicting emotions swirling in his eyes and hear the frustrated rage in his voice when he rasped, "You've got it fucking wrong, but I don't have time to discuss that with you right now. I'm asking you to trust me."

Mia wanted to, desperately ached to, but her broken heart wouldn't allow her to take the chance on making a third, life-altering mistake. "I'm sorry, Chief. I'm done with trusting the wrong men." She twisted free of his hold and dashed behind the shop to sit at the picnic table, keeping her back to the yard as she dialed Bob's number. His cheerful greeting shattered the fragile hold on her composure and she crumbled.

"Bob, I-I need you."

"I OUGHT to beat the shit out of you for this," Nolan snarled at Chuck, the image of Mia's ravaged, pain-filled face swimming in his head. "Why didn't you wait?"

"The warrant came through, and I couldn't chance her getting wind of Barry talking to us this morning. Quit thinking with your dick and help us," his ex-boss snapped back.

"Barry fucking cleared her, you know that." He refused to aid them in ransacking Mia's place. He had hurt her enough.

"In words, yes. But we still need proof since the inventory she ordered that we pulled over was loaded with cocaine. And we need leverage to pull Barry's contact from him."

"The kid's too scared to give him up." Nolan ached to return to Mia and force her to listen to him. But until he'd taken her statement and they could persuade Barry to reveal his contact, the best way to protect her would be to keep a professional distance for a day or two. No longer. He couldn't abide staying away from her longer than that. The consequences to the case be damned. It tore at him the way she'd backed off, her pale face and tormented green eyes reflecting pain and confusion. It was a look that would haunt him for months, and a situation he needed to rectify as soon as possible.

Chuck's look turned grim. "We'll get him into protective custody. He'll talk eventually, if he ever wants his life back."

It sounded cold and ruthless, but they both knew it was the only way to get these stupid, scared kids to cooperate. "Fuck, but I do not miss this," Nolan swore. Bob Templeton arrived, and he breathed a sigh of relief Mia's friend and lawyer was here to help shoulder her burden. "I'm going back to the hospital to talk to

Barry before I take Mia's statement." He didn't wait for Chuck's approval, just stormed off with a desperate need to right this wrong as fast as possible clawing at his insides.

"WHAT IF HE WAKES UP? We're fucking screwed!"

Clifton ushered Sanchez out of the barn, away from the ears of the rest of his hired hands. News of their connection at Greenleaf overdosing had already reached him and he'd been working hard to liquefy as many assets as possible while making plans to get out of the country. "We are if you can't get a grip on yourself," he snapped, wishing it was Raoul lying in a coma. At least then he would shut up. "The kid's wasted, quit fretting over what *might* happen and get the rest of the shed tonight. With the en route shipment confiscated, that'll clear our inventory, leaving nothing for the Feds to find if they end up here."

"It's getting too dicey. I want out." Sanchez crossed his arms, stubbornness tightening his face as he glared at Clifton.

"After you deliver what's left." He refused to allow Sanchez to leave him holding the bag. The damn imbecile could just suck up one more delivery before bailing. It looked like he would be cutting his losses sooner than he'd planned. It almost killed him to put the spread up for auction, but that was better than going to prison.

"I'll get it done tonight then we're done."

Fine by me, he thought as he returned to the barn to see to the beloved horses he wouldn't own much longer.

MIA WALKED out of the interrogation room with her head high despite the roiling queasiness that wouldn't abate even though the worst part of her ordeal seemed to be over. She heard

Nolan's deep voice talking to someone and then the door close behind her, just as it had on her fragile hopes.

"We'll follow you home," Bob offered as he and Dee walked with her down the hall.

"No, thank you, both of you. But I'd rather be alone now. Please."

"Mia." Dee wrapped her arms around her and it took every ounce of what control she still possessed not to break down. "Come home with us tonight. You shouldn't be alone."

"I may as well get used to it again. Thanks, but I want to go home. I'll call you tomorrow."

Mia paused in the waiting room until her friends drove away. Swiveling from the front window, her gaze landed on the deputy's desk, and the picture lying face up on it.

"Something wrong, Ms. Reynolds?" Hank asked, his heart going out to the pale-faced woman who'd been through so much that day.

Pointing to the photo of Sanchez, she said, "I know him. He works for Clifton Birmingham."

"He does? We haven't been able to ID him." Hank picked up a pen and notepad. "What's his name?"

"Sanchez. Creepy guy." A thought just occurred to her. "I saw him with Barry at the County Line, but Barry swore they didn't know each other."

"Thanks, that's a big help. I'll pass it on to the Chief."

Mia nodded and walked out to her truck, the lead weight pressing on her chest still making it difficult to breathe. She wondered how long it would take her to recover this time. It was dark by the time she returned to the nursery after spending a grueling two hours at the police precinct. Thank goodness for the numbness that had taken over her body that afternoon and still shielded her from the full reality of the day's stunning revelations. Bob and Dee had taken up a seat on each side of her while

Nolan drilled her, their unwavering support a debt she could never repay.

Bob tried convincing her before she spoke with Nolan that he was just doing his job, had insisted Nolan's aloofness was necessary to avoid accusations of preferential treatment. She'd shoved aside his explanations, too tired and devastated to think of anything except crawling into bed.

Drew and Donny had also been brought in, and Nolan had given her the only good news of the day, telling her neither was directly involved with dealing drugs. Hearing about how both knew about Barry's use and dealings and had covered for him was hard enough to cope with. She hated to imagine she'd been gullible enough to employ three criminals. Their assurances she knew nothing of Barry's activities or the drugs funneled into the state via her inventory had gone a long way in clearing her, along with the search that turned up nothing. Sliding out of the truck, Mia thought she should feel a sense of relief her ordeal was over, but she continued to feel very little.

The Feds hadn't bothered flipping on the outdoor lights when they'd finished tearing up her property, so she stumbled her way through the dark toward the stairs. At least their thoughtlessness kept her from seeing the destruction from their search, and of her dreams.

A sudden sound shattered the stillness of the yard and penetrated her foggy head as she placed a hand on the stair banister. Before she could turn, a hard hand covered her mouth with a damp cloth, startling her into dropping her purse. Icy fear twisted around her heart as she struggled to breathe, the nauseous odor invading her senses working to dim her vision as she slumped into unconsciousness.

MIA ROUSED to groggy awareness with a metallic taste in her

mouth and spasmodic trembling in her limbs. The sweet smell of straw filled her nostrils as she struggled to open her gritty eyes. Blinking in rapid movement, her blurred vision cleared enough for her to make out the wood walls enclosing her in a small, empty structure with a sliver of daylight filtering through the cracks. How long had she been out? She tried and failed to control her erratic pulse, the panic rioting through her generating needles of edgy panic stabbing at her abdomen. Rolling from her side to her back, she attempted to lower her aching right arm and met with manacled resistance. Unlike the instant lust she'd grown accustomed to feeling when bound, this time terror set her insides to quivering. After a few minutes of sweat-inducing exertion, she managed to sit up using her free arm, her vision clearing enough to make out the form of the man leaning against the far wall, his cold black gaze threatening to bore a hole right through her.

"What have you done?" she croaked past her parched throat.

Sanchez pushed away from the wall and stomped across the dirty, hay-strewn floor, each step matching the menace his eyes aimed at her. "This is all your fault. If you hadn't gone snooping after seeing me with the kid, no one would be the wiser."

Mia's befuddled brain slowly kicked into gear, but with clarity came an increase in fear. "You're his connection."

"I knew you'd figure it out, so I tried taking off. Only the fucking Feds are everywhere and so is my picture now." Reaching down, he hauled her to her feet and shook her. "I was just going to hold on to you until I got clear, but now it's too late. Now, you're my ticket out of here."

"Where's Clifton?" she croaked on a gasp as he released her to lean against the wall for much needed support.

Sanchez sneered. "Cowardly bastard snuck out of here last night after he saw me hauling your ass in here. I hope they fry him."

She wasn't sure if he meant the Feds or the drug lords and

didn't care. If the man who had been portraying himself as an upstanding, law-abiding citizen all these years was involved, he deserved to go down. And then everything seemed to shift into place as the final cobwebs drifted out of her head. Birmingham had approached her with his lucrative landscaping contract one short week after she'd hired Barry. God, how could she have been so pathetically ignorant all these weeks?

"Barry snuck the crates transporting the drugs off the flatbeds and into the delivery truck and then delivered them out here, didn't he?"

"Give the woman a prize. Right under your nose, bitch, and you'd still be in the dark if it wasn't for us running into you coming out of the bar."

Mia didn't know where her bravado popped up from, all she knew was that she was sick at heart and tired of being taken advantage of. Only, she realized it was her reluctance to be completely open and forthcoming with Nolan that kept him from learning about Sanchez before now. Honesty forced her to admit if she'd pointed him out at the bar the last time they were there, and mentioned seeing him with Barry, he might have put two and two together before this, definitely before she had. *That wasn't the only time I threw up a wall between us.*

The chop-chop of an approaching helicopter caught both of their attention and a surge of hope rushed through her. Had she been able to stand here and confront Sanchez because deep down, she'd known Nolan would come for her? As the rumble of numerous vehicles pouring onto the surrounding grounds shook beneath her feet, she knew it bore thinking about. Later.

"Fuck! I should have had more time."

Voices filtered through the thin walls and Sanchez's face darkened even more as he nailed her with his frigid gaze. Reaching behind him, he pulled a gun from his waist, yanked Mia in front of him, put the pistol to her temple and dragged her out of the barn into the bright, early morning sun before halting in front of a semi-circle of flashing, federal and state law-enforcement vehicles.

Instant, blinding terror clouded Mia's senses and hysteria threatened to overtake the relative calm she'd maintained until now. With her life flashing before her eyes, she realized how much Nolan meant to her, how she may have let Peter's betrayal blind her to the truth of his involvement with putting her nursery under surveillance. His rough, demanding, arrogant voice broke through the panic consuming her as she struggled in Sanchez's bruising hold. The same tone that would either make her grit her teeth in annoyance or send her pulse skyrocketing now soothed her raw, frayed nerves and calmness settled over her like a comforting embrace.

"Let her go, Sanchez."

NOLAN HUNKERED down behind the open door of his cruiser, aimed his rifle and held his breath. His heart still threatened to pound right out of his chest and a ball of terror still clogged his throat. He hadn't learned of Mia's knowledge of Sanchez until several hours after she'd mentioned it to Hank. After passing it on to Chuck, he couldn't wait a second longer to return to the nursery, tie her to the bed and torment her into listening to him. He'd been in a state of rage and panic ever since he found her purse at the bottom of the stairs to her apartment and Mia nowhere around. If they hadn't tracked down Clifton Birmingham preparing to fly out of the country from a small, private airport, they'd still be searching for her. The fucker started singing before Nolan had even whipped out his cuffs.

Nolan's gut twisted into a painful ball when Sanchez stepped out of the dilapidated barn using Mia as a human shield. He could detect the terror reflected on her face, even from this distance. Her shorts and legs were dirty, her face streaked and flushed, and straw clung to her hair. He'd say disheveled and smudged was how he liked her best, but not in this case. Keeping a beaded eye and direct aim at the bastard's forehead, he prepared to pull the trigger if Sanchez didn't cooperate.

"Not gonna happen. Back off until I'm gone, then I'll tell you where you can come pick her up," Sanchez answered with a tighter press of the gun nozzle to Mia's head, her wince turning Nolan's vision red. She'd have a bruise there tomorrow, and for that alone, he could kill him.

The helicopter carrying even more backup landed and he started to bring the megaphone back up when a look came over Mia's face that turned his blood to ice water in his veins. Normally that scowl stirred his lust, but not this time. Annoyance with her whole situation must've surpassed her fear because one second she was struggling against her captor and the next she went limp, sagging in his one-arm hold like a rag doll.

Surprised, Sanchez relaxed his grip as Nolan tensed and curled his finger over the trigger. The next second, Mia rammed her bent head up and back, smacking Sanchez in the nose and drawing a gush of blood. The gun wavered and Nolan pulled his trigger, putting a neat bullet hole in her captor's forehead. As he toppled over backward from instant death, Nolan rushed forward to snatch Mia up in his trembling arms.

She clung to him, her body shaking, her ragged breathing fanning his neck, her quiet tears soaking his shirt. Love swamped him so hard his head swam. It had been Mia for ten years, ever since that day on the street and some indefinable emotion sparked between them that neither cared to analyze at the time.

"God damn it," he breathed before declaring in a furious whisper, "I love you, Mia."

Chapter 12

Mia leaned her head back against the headrest as Nolan drove her home from the precinct. After taking a quick shower in the station's miniscule bathroom, she'd spent two hours talking to the Feds with her hand enfolded in Nolan's tight grip. Without that lifeline, she doubted she could have held up against the mental exhaustion. She'd misjudged him, she knew and regretted that now. Somehow, she would find a way to make it up to him and return his declaration. Her well-laid plans to remain single and avoid heartache went out the window the first time he touched her and drove her to heights of ecstasy she'd never imagined, only she'd been too stubborn and blind to see it.

Right now, all she could think about was the ruins of her business awaiting her as she wondered how she would ever bounce back after this. Would people blame her even though the Feds had exonerated her? She shuddered to think they might, and despaired over where to go from here. It had taken her years to build up the nursery, to garner enough support and business until she needed to hire extra help. Now look at where one employee had left her.

"You're being awfully quiet," Nolan said with a quick glance her way. "Think about this instead of the last twenty-four hours. I want you to move in with me. We can go to my place now and you can rest while I pack up some of your belongings."

She shook her head, a small laugh emerging from her tight throat. "You could try *asking.*"

"That doesn't work with you. Telling, browbeating you first, and if that doesn't work I can always strap you down and withhold your climaxes until you agree. In fact, I might prefer that method."

Mia warmed from head to toe, the last of the terrifying coldness that had invaded her body since the Feds arrived on her doorstep yesterday thawing under his hot look. She opened her mouth to tell him how she felt as he turned onto her property, but the jam-packed parking lot and multitude of people awaiting her rendered her speechless. A lump formed in her throat and wouldn't budge as he pulled over and she noticed they weren't just waiting but working to set her place to rights.

"What… what's all this?" she stuttered, tears pooling in her eyes as she reached for the door handle with a hand that shook.

"You're well liked, sweetheart." Nolan came around and took her elbow when she stumbled on the first step toward the yard.

Her eyes flew up to his. "Did you arrange this?"

He shrugged. "Me, Bob, Dee, Trish and a few others. It didn't take much, a few phone calls and word spread like wildfire. We should have you up and running again in no time."

In a daze, Mia took in everyone willing to help her out with no questions asked. A soft cry spilled past her trembling lips when she spotted her boys among them, Cory flipping her one of his cocky grins before turning back to repotting a large aloe vera plant, and Casey sending her a thumbs up as he watered a flatbed of newly re-planted catmint flowers.

"Come over here a minute." Nolan squeezed her hand and tugged her toward a long table where she recognized Mrs.

MacGregor serving beverages. Remembering her dirty clothes, she balked at meeting his mother formally for the first time looking as she did, but should have known he wouldn't let her hide. "Mom, this is Mia."

"Oh, you poor dear." Dashing around the table, the older woman enveloped Mia in her round arms and hugged her. "I was so relieved when Nolan let me know he found you and you were okay."

"Thank you, Mrs. MacGregor." Uncomfortable, she gently disengaged from the clinging, well-meaning woman and stepped back only to exchange his mother's arms for Nolan's.

"Do you need help here, Mom?"

"Oh, heavens no. I can handle pouring out drinks. Before I forget, Mia. I have to tell you how much I've loved the flowers and plants from your shop. I keep telling Nolan no more, but he doesn't listen. They always brighten my day, and my house. I envy you your green thumb."

"Thank you," she responded before twisting and glaring at Nolan. "I didn't know they were for you."

Unperturbed, he shrugged and bent to whisper in her ear. "I told you to trust me."

"Rub it in, why don't you?" she muttered, red-faced.

"I intend to. Mom, I'll check back with you shortly."

"You two go on. Everyone will set this place to rights in no time."

They started toward the greenhouse when Annie, Mia's accountant, strolled up carrying a white flowered fern bush in her arms.

"Hey, Mia," she greeted them. "Instead of putting this back up for sale, mind if I set it aside? It'd look great in a corner of my back yard."

"No, go ahead, in fact, just take it, Annie, as a—" Her voice caught, her overwhelming gratitude forcing her to pause before she finished saying, "—thank you."

"Nonsense, hon. I'm more than happy to buy it. I'll set it by the checkout."

She watched Annie walk away as if nothing had happened, her unquestioning support and friendship meaning so much, as did that of everyone else lending a hand. Nolan had joined a few men in unloading dirt from a pickup and as Mia turned to pitch in, she once more stumbled to an abrupt halt, this time at seeing Peter sliding out of his fancy BMW. Squaring her shoulders, she vowed not to let anything he said ruin this special day for her. It was more than time to put the past away.

Not believing the look of concern on his face when he reached her, she shook a finger at him. "Look, if you've come—"

He held up a hand, his face softening with what could only be called regret. "First, are you all right? When I heard…" He swallowed and looked away before facing her again. "I'm sorry for what you've been through, Mia, and for what I put you through. You of all people didn't deserve that. I've accepted a job offer in Taos. Tami and I are moving there in a few weeks. If you're interested, I'm willing to sell the house back to you at a price below market value."

Good grief, will the day's stunning surprises never end? Mia gave herself a mental headshake and met him halfway in his attempt to set aside their differences. "What's done is done, Peter." She glanced at Nolan and a wave of love punched her chest; not the small pop she used to feel for Peter, but a wallop that threatened to buckle her knees. Thinking of living with him, she shook her head. "Thanks, but I have a house to move into. Good luck in Taos."

Nodding toward Nolan, Peter asked, "You're happy, with him?"

Oh yeah, he made her happy. "I love him," she returned, tickled by a flare of inner triumph. *Look at that, I didn't choke on the words.*

"That's good. Mind if I stick around, maybe help our sons with what they're doing?"

"Knock yourself out." She waved him their way and then turned her back on her past.

NOLAN WAITED until Mia hugged Dee and Bob, the last to leave, before locking the shop and tossing the bag he'd packed for her in his cruiser. They were both wiped out, but every uprooted plant and upended planter had been put to rights and the volunteers fed when food arrived from the diner and the local deli sandwich shop. Now all that was left to do would be to set Mia straight on a few things.

"I thought we'd just crash here tonight," she griped when he opened the passenger door and ushered her in his vehicle. "I'm exhausted, and you must be too."

Sliding behind the wheel, he started the engine and pulled out. "I am, but I want my bed, and you in it."

"Oh, okay."

She may not have agreed so fast if she knew he intended a short scene before letting her rest. Wasting no time after ushering her inside his house, he led her down the hall, the crestfallen look on her face as he escorted her past his playroom and straight into the bedroom priceless. "How many times, sweetheart, have I asked you to trust me?" He sat on the bed and his hands went to the waist of her shorts, the chagrin filling her green eyes revealing she knew exactly what he was referring to.

"I've been meaning to apologize for accusing you of using me but haven't had a chance." A startled yelp burst from her as he shoved her shorts and panties down and hauled her over his lap, the first swat reddening her right cheek to a bright hue.

"That's a nice start." He smacked her left buttock and then the right again, enjoying the feel of her soft skin heating under his hand, hearing her cries and seeing her ass wiggle from the growing discomfort he was heaping upon her.

"But not enough." A sob broke free as he peppered her backside with a volley of sharp slaps, her malleable globes shifting and clenching under his hand. "Not only did your distrust send you running from me, but kept me from learning more about the man who caused you such grief. That," he blistered one sit-spot, "is not acceptable. But," he hit the opposite tender area next, "that's not what this is about."

"It's not?" Mia flipped her head up, her flushed face clouded with confusion and then consternation when he reached for the hairbrush he'd purposely left on the bedside table.

"No." He didn't elaborate until he delivered several blows using the wooden back, the loud smacks and her cries reverberating in the room. By the time he stopped, her buttocks were bright crimson, her slit a glistening enticement and her wracking sobs a sign of surrender. Flipping the brush around in his hand, he lightly scratched her tender, abused skin with the bristles, her entire body shuddering with her low moan. Tossing the brush aside, he turned her in his arms and held her close. "There, all done. You trusted me with your body, Mia, but not the part of you I want and need most." He gazed into her tear-drenched eyes and placed his hand over her pounding heart.

Framing his face with her hands, she returned his solemn gaze and whispered the words he needed to hear, "God help me, I love both Master Nolan and Chief Nolan, with all my heart."

"About fucking time," he growled before covering her trembling mouth with his.

The End

BJ Wane

I live in the Midwest with my husband and our two dogs, a Poodle/Pyrenees mix and an Irish Water Spaniel. I love dogs, spending time with my daughter, babysitting her two dogs, reading and working puzzles. We have traveled extensively throughout the states, Canada and just once overseas, but I much prefer being a homebody. I worked for a while writing articles for a local magazine but soon found my interest in writing for myself peaking. My first book was strictly spanking erotica, but I slowly evolved to writing erotic romance with an emphasis on spanking. I love hearing from readers and can be reached here: bjwane@cox.net.

Recent accolades include: 5 star, Top Pick review from The Romance Reviews for *Blindsided*, 5 star review from Long & Short Reviews for Hannah & The Dom Next Door, which was also voted Erotic Romance of the Month on LASR, and my most recent title, Her Master At Last, took two spots on top 100 lists in BDSM erotica and Romantic erotica in less than a week!

Visit her Facebook page
https://www.facebook.com/bj.wane
Visit her blog here
bjwane.blogspot.com

Don't miss these exciting titles by BJ Wane and Blushing Books!

Single Titles

Claiming Mia

Virginia Bluebloods Series
Blindsided, Book 1
Bind Me To You, Book 2
Surrender To Me, Book 3
Blackmailed, Book 4
Bound By Two, Book 5
Determined to Master: Complete Series

Murder On Magnolia Island Trilogy
Logan - Book 1
Hunter - Book 2
Ryder - Book 3

Miami Masters
Bound and Saved - Book One
Master Me, Please - Book Two
Mastering Her Fear - Book Three
Bound to Submit - Book Four
His to Master and Own - Book Five
Theirs to Master - Book Six

Masters of the Castle
Witness Protection Program
(Controlling Carlie)

Connect with BJ Wane
bjwane.blogspot.com